"My man's got a Winchester on your partner, big man."

"If you don't send down the girl, he's gonna blow off the top of his head."

"Son of a bitch," Raider grumbled under his breath.

Doc's unmistakable voice rolled over the notch. "Don't do it, Raider. Don't give her up..."

"What'll it be, Pinkerton?" cried Sturgess.

"Okay, Sturgess, you win. Stay right where you are and I'll bring her down. You got to promise you won't shoot us."

"I promise," came the reply.

Raider saw the corner of a hat brim sticking out behind a rock. He tossed a boulder over the edge, watching as it crashed into the stones and boulders below. As the heavy rock fell, it loosened other stony debris. A rumbling filled the air as the rockslide began.

"It's rainin'," Raider said. "Rainin' rocks on Harv Sturgess. I just hope he brought along his slicker."

J.D. HARDIN

CARSON CITY COLT

BERKLEY BOOKS, NEW YORK

CARSON CITY COLT

A Berkley Book/published by arrangement with
the author

PRINTING HISTORY
Berkley edition/January 1986

ISBN: 0-425-07969-4

A BERKLEY BOOK ® TM 757,375

Berkley Books are published by The Berkley Publishing Group,
200 Madison Avenue, New York, N.Y. 10016.
The name "BERKLEY" and the stylized "B" with design are trademarks
belonging to Berkley Publishing Corporation.

PRINTED IN THE UNITED STATES OF AMERICA

**Dedicated to
Peter Happny, Blacksmith**

CHAPTER ONE

"Where the hell is Doc?"

Raider stood on a high mesa, peering to the south, watching for signs of his partner. They had been separated when Raider grabbed the woman and rode north to get away from Harv Sturgess and his men. Now the sun was hanging low over the Arizona plain, threatening to shroud the countryside in thick shadows. The big Pinkerton detective from Arkansas gazed up at the blue and orange sky, wondering if there was Someone up there watching over his partner.

"It ain't a good time for Doc to be wanderin' around alone."

He turned back toward the woman. She sat cross-legged on the ground, holding the reins of the gray gelding. Her brown eyes were cast downward, away from Raider. Hair as black as coal and skin the color of creamed coffee. The remnants of a calico dress barely covered her full bosom.

Raider fought the urge to touch her. It wasn't the time or place. Not with the Sturgess gang nearby.

"You all right, lady?"

She turned the brown eyes on him. Her thick lips were parted. Raider didn't know how to read her.

1

"I asked if you were all right, woman?"

"Yes. I am alive and away from Harv Sturgess. Thank you."

Her shoulders trembled. Raider slipped off his denim jacket and draped it over her to stave off the impending chill of night. The woman grabbed his hand and kissed his palm. Her scent lingered on the still air, almost paralyzing Raider. He drew away and looked down at her.

"What do they call you?"

"Angelica."

"Can I call you Angel?"

"If you wish."

Raider met her eyes for a moment. She was grateful for her rescue. He wondered what she might do to thank him. He shook his head and pulled his Winchester out of the scabbard on the gray's saddle. As he jacked a cartridge into the chamber, the woman stood up.

"Why do you pull away from me, cowboy? Don't you like me? Or are you ashamed to touch me because I am half Mexican?"

Raider rested the Winchester in the crook of his arm. "Angel, I don't think you're catchin' on to the trouble we're in. Your old beau is probably ridin' wild asses all over this territory lookin' for you and me. And somewhere out there my partner is all by his lonesome. Doc's a pretty smart old boy, but he might not have a chance against your boyfriend and his—"

"Harv Sturgess is nothing to me!" she cried. "I hate him. He held me against my will. I never—"

Raider put his free hand on her shoulder. "Shh, don't get all riled up. I know you was kidnapped by Sturgess. And I know who hired him. The man's already in custody in Phoenix. We just got to get you back so you can testify against him."

"Kiss me, cowboy. Just kiss me."

Raider lowered his mouth to her thick lips. She threw her arms around him and sought his tongue with a hungry mouth. Raider let himself enjoy her kiss for a moment and then pushed her away.

Angelica tossed her long hair. "I hate you," she cried. "I hate you as much as Harv Sturgess."

Raider laughed. "Yeah? Maybe I ought give your ass back to him. Would you like that?"

She put a delicate hand to her throat.

"Don't worry," Raider said. "I ain't gonna do it. I'm just tellin' you that we got to concentrate on other things now. Maybe when all of this is over we can . . . I mean . . . hell, you're a damned pretty woman."

She frowned and began to cry. Raider reached into his boot and withdrew a .32-caliber derringer. He put the small pistol in her hand.

"Take this in case we get treed," he said.

She nodded. If there was one thing women understood, Raider thought, it was survival. A female mountain lion was just as much trouble as her mate. Especially if you got her cornered.

He turned back toward the plain, wishing he had Doc's telescope. The air grew colder as the sun dipped behind a low mountain range to the west. Where the hell was Doc? Had he been able to escape on that damned mule of his? Raider's stomach churned like he had swallowed a pear cactus. He was beginning to think he had done the wrong thing by running with the girl. But they needed her in Phoenix. She was going to send several influential people to the territorial prison in Yuma.

"Do you see your partner?" Angelica asked.

"No. Not yet."

"What are we going to do?"

Raider exhaled a caustic breath. "Lady, I wish I knew. I figure we're a day's ride from Phoenix, but I don't want to leave Doc out here by hisself. I don't think he can . . . God-oh . . ."

Angelica stepped up beside him. Her eyes grew wide when she saw the dust rising on the shadowy horizon. Reflexively, she drew in closer to the big man with the Winchester in his hands.

"Is that your partner, cowboy?"

Raider shook his head. "One man don't make that much commotion. I'm guessin' that your old boyfriend picked up our trail."

"Are we going to—"

"Run," Raider said.

Doc had some saying about valor, but Raider couldn't remember the quote exactly. He grabbed Angelica's waist and lifted her onto the gray. The animal was lathered and tired. Raider rubbed the horse's muzzle.

"Don't quit on me now, partner."

He jumped into the saddle in front of Angelica. She wrapped her arms around his waist, but Raider didn't feel them. He took an extra moment to peer southward, making sure the dust was no mirage. When he detected the faint echo of distant hooves, he spurred the gray and started west. Their best chance was to head for the mountains. If they could hide long enough, maybe Sturgess would quit looking for them. Raider didn't like the idea of facing six-guns with his Winchester and a scared woman.

The gray galloped toward the half-circle of the sun behind the mountains. It was going to be a cold night, and with Sturgess on their tails they wouldn't be able to risk a fire. Raider's limbs were suddenly stiff. As he rode headlong into dusk, he realized that his troubles might not be anything compared to the fate met by his partner, Doc Weatherbee.

Doc Weatherbee listed in the saddle of a black gelding, trying to maintain his balance as he rode north with Harv Sturgess and his men. Doc's hands were tied behind him, so he had to use his legs to keep himself in the stirrups. When Raider had grabbed the girl, Doc had covered him with his .38 Diamondback, firing and killing two of Sturgess's men. But as Raider escaped, Doc felt a slug creasing his forehead, knocking him unconscious. Dried blood covered the remains of his shredded suit coat. He felt weak, but he was sure he would survive—if Sturgess didn't finish him off.

The four horses stirred dust in front of Doc, gagging him as he tried to breathe. He lowered his face to catch the cloud on the narrow brim of his pearl-gray derby but found that he could not maintain his balance with his head down. He was greatly relieved when the horses stopped in the cool shadows of twilight. Doc watched as Harv Sturgess dismounted and looked at the trail.

Sturgess was a surprisingly dapper outlaw. He wore the black suit and Stetson of a riverboat gambler. He tugged at his string tie as he examined the path. He wasn't a well-known criminal, never having reached the status of the James boys or the Youngers. But Sturgess was the kind of obscure vermin that did the dirty work for powerful, unscrupulous men.

Sturgess looked up from the trail, gazing north. He turned back to his men and nodded. A filthy man known as Little hopped out of the saddle to confirm his boss's sighting. Doc felt a chill when Little glanced back up at him. The man's ratty countenance was contorted in a hateful grimace. Doc had seen the same face on a child's hideous jack-o'-lantern.

"The other Pinkerton is headin' this way," Little said. "I say we kill this one now. Hell, he's half dead already."

Sturgess shook his head. "We need him, Little."

"For what?"

"For a trade," Sturgess replied. "Weatherbee for the girl. That big man ain't gonna let his partner die."

He was looking right at Doc, who forced a smile. "I assure you," Doc said, "my partner will never give her up. Not even if you offer my life for hers. Nor would I tell him to do so."

Little drew an old Navy Colt .36 and thumbed back the hammer. He pointed it at Doc, but Sturgess knocked his hand away. Doc felt the ice growing on his spine. The small man with the reaper's face snorted at his boss.

"He's right, Harv. That big 'un ain't gonna let her go. We're gonna have to run 'em down and kill both of 'em."

Sturgess pushed Little toward his horse. "Mount up, boy. We've got to ride. They're probably headin' for the mountains, and we'll have a lot of trouble trackin' them in the dark."

"What about this Pinkerton dandy?" Little asked.

Sturgess frowned. "Can't you see what I'm tryin' to tell you, Little? We ain't gonna let either one of them go. As far as I can see, we have to kill all three of them sooner or later. But this one's worth more alive right now."

"Yeah, yeah. I see what you mean. Hear that, Pinkerton? You're a dead man, boy. Har, har. A goddamn dead man."

Doc raised an eyebrow and mustered his courage. "Mr. Little, if I am forced to inhabit a world populated by people like you, then I prefer to make my way into the afterlife. It is unfortunate, however, that I must leave this earth at the hands of a scoundrel such as yourself."

Little was scratching his head. "What the hell is he talking about?"

Sturgess jumped into the saddle. "Shut up, boy, and ride."

The horses pounded the turf toward the vague rise of the mountains to the west. Doc thought about his mule, Judith, who had been left behind at Sturgess's camp. He might never see her again. He thought about his partner, trying to remember something bad about Raider so he would not wax sentimental with his demise so close. But nothing unpleasant would come to mind.

Doc smiled suddenly. Raider was his last hope. The big man from Arkansas had a remarkable talent for surfacing at precisely the right time. With guns in hand, Raider was more than a match for the likes of Harv Sturgess. And if he lost his temper, he might be able to handle all four of them.

Raider guided the gray into a narrow ravine between two rocky slopes. The sun was completely gone, but a crescent moon had risen to partially light the way. For the first time since they had left the mesa, he was aware of the woman's presence behind him. Her breasts pressed against his back, taking his mind away from important matters—like saving their lives.

"Where are we?" she asked in a soft voice.

"I ain't sure. Just keep quiet while I find us a place to rest."

The gray's hooves splashed in a noisy stream that ran along the bottom of the ravine. Raider was hoping to find some sort of cave or crevice where they might be able to build a fire. Angelica was shivering behind him. He tried not to entertain thoughts of keeping her warm with his own body.

"I'm hungry," she said in a tired voice.

"There might be some dried jerky in my saddlebag," Raider replied. "I got to find a place to sleep first."

"Can we have a fire? I'm freezing."

"Just hang on as long as you can. I'll see what I can do."

Raider dismounted, walking the gray along the stream. The ravine widened as they went further into the shadows. He spotted a sandy patch of sediment where another rivulet emptied into the larger stream. There was a rift between the rocky slopes of the crevass. It seemed to be big enough for two people to slip in and hide.

"Wait here," he said.

"But I don't want—"

"Just do it!"

Raider drew his Colt .45 Peacemaker and slid into the narrow opening. His feet splashed in the runoff water from the mountains above. He felt lichens and moss beneath the soles of his boots. As the crack narrowed into an impassable crevice, Raider gave up and turned back. He felt his way along the rock until his hand went into a dark recess. There was an indentation in the wall of the crevice. It was barely big enough for two people, but it would do.

Angelica was still in the saddle when he splashed back into the ravine.

"You were gone a damned long time, cowboy."

Raider pulled her out of the saddle. "Quit your yappin'."

He carried her into the crack between the rocks, depositing her in the weathered stone alcove. She crouched down and leaned back against the mossy wall. Then she screamed and stood up, crying out that there was something underneath her. Raider reached down and picked up a harmless water snake. He tossed the snake into the shadows.

"It won't hurt you, girl. Now you just stay here while I scrounge up some firewood. I don't think it would hurt to have a fire back here. Sturgess ain't gonna see us unless he gets real lucky in the dark."

"He's not the lucky kind," Angelica replied.

"I hope you're right, Angel. I sure as hell hope you're right."

Raider stomped toward the gray, wondering if there was something that a big man could do for a living that didn't involve running like a savage through the cold night. He entertained thoughts of a warm hearth and a little woman stirring a kettle of stew. But he knew those thoughts would pass—if he ever got out of the ravine alive.

"We ain't never gonna find them in the dark," said Harv Sturgess.

They had reched the mountains faster than Doc had figured. Little was a great tracker, one of the best Doc had ever seen. Would he be able to determine the signs from Raider's trail in the dark?

"I can find them, Harv," Little said. "I know I can."

Sturgess shook his head. "No. We make camp here for

tonight. At first light we'll pick up the trail."

"I'm tellin' you, Harv, I can do it. Just follow me."

"Who's runnin' this gang?" Sturgess said.

The fire went out of Little's voice. "You, Harv. You're the one who's runnin' things. I'm just wantin' to help. Hell, you and me go a long way back. I'd never—"

"Cut the soap," Sturgess replied. "Lamont, you and Billy make a fire."

The other two men climbed out of their saddles. Little was hovering next to Sturgess. Doc wondered if they were going to take him off his horse. He could not get down by himself, not with his hands tied behind him.

"You sure you want to make a fire, Harv?" Little asked. "I mean, that other Pinkerton might see it and ride down on us."

Sturgess tipped back his Stetson. "If he does ride down, that means we don't have to find him. Besides, we got him outnumbered, and with his partner here in tow, I don't think he'll risk it."

Little looked up at Doc. "Think he'll risk it, Weatherbee?"

"I think nothing," Doc replied.

"Smart-alecky bastard," Little said. He turned to Sturgess. "Let me go after the big man and the girl, Harv."

"In the dark?"

Little grinned. "I learned how to track from a Injun named Red Horse. I can find anything, anytime. Let me do it, Harv."

Sturgess was hesitant. "Little, that's a Pinkerton out there. It ain't like you're chasin' an ordinary lawman."

"He's right," Doc said.

"Shut up," Little cried. "Let me go, Harv. I'll come back if I don't find him."

"I wouldn't advise it," Doc rejoined.

Sturgess looked up at Doc. "All right, Little, you go on after the big man. Cut his throat with your huntin' knife if you find him."

Little gave a goblin's cry and lurched off into the night. Doc was shaking his head and frowning. Sturgess pulled him off the black, causing Doc to hit the ground with a heavy thud. Sturgess hovered over him.

"You don't want my boy to find your partner, do you, Weatherbee?"

Doc grunted and rolled over to face his captor. "On the

contrary, Mr. Sturgess. I hope he finds Raider immediately. If he does, he might just be in for an unwelcome surprise."

Raider had a hard time finding a place to tie the gray. He finally wrapped the reins around a small boulder and wedged it into a deep crack. For a moment he had considered letting the gray run free, saddle and all, to make Harv Sturgess think he had been thrown or killed. But from what he had seen of Sturgess, he knew that the dapper bandit would make a sustained effort to find him, even in the mountains.

When the gray was secured, Raider removed the saddlebags and started back through the crevice. He found Angelica drawn up into a ball, shivering against the moss-covered stone. She was too fine a woman to be subjected to such harsh treatment. Her brown eyes flashed in the darkness, but Raider could not see the desperate desire in her face. He slipped down beside her.

"Sorry I was gone so long, Angel."

She scooted next to him, pressing her body against his. Raider did not push her away. He was almost as cold and scared as the lady. Reaching into his saddlebag, he withdrew two sticks of dried meat. Angelica grabbed the jerky from his hands and started to gnaw ravenously.

"My God, cowboy, I've never tasted anything so good. If only there was some way to keep warm."

Raider ignored the inviting tone of her voice. He had to keep what little strength he had left. Angelica might drain him if he let her. He bit into the jerky, thinking that he would sell half his soul for a cup of Doc's coffee.

"We need a blanket," Angelica said.

"Well, we ain't got one."

"The horse blanket."

Raider shook his head. "It stinks too much."

"I want to be warm. I'd sleep in that horse's belly if I thought—"

"We got to keep the gray saddled," he replied. "We might have to run again, quick. Hell, we might oughta keep runnin' in the night."

"Can we have a fire at least?" she asked, slapping her shoulders.

"There's nothin' to burn in this ravine. If we . . ."

Some stones fell down over the front of the cave. Raider's body tensed. His hand was full of the Colt. He had drawn it out of reflex.

Angelica trembled against him. "What is—"

He put his hand over her mouth, holding his breath. Did Sturgess have a man good enough to find them in the dark? More stones rattling outside. He had left his Winchester in the scabbard on the gray. It was a damned fool mistake, even if he was lost in the middle of nowhere.

The gray whinnied and began to beat the ground with its hooves. Raider leaned forward, scrambling to his feet. He had not expected a showdown so soon. He stepped out into the darkness in time to hear the banshee cry of a mountain lion. His black eyes lifted toward the sky to see the shadow of a cougar against the moon. The big cat leapt onto the gray's neck, clawing and chewing with a feline death grip.

Raider had to risk a shot, even if Sturgess heard him. He fired the Colt just as the gray went down. He thought he had missed the cat. He fired again to see the cougar's angry face in the flame from the muzzle blast. The cat left the horse's body and came straight for him.

When Raider fired again, the cat was in the air, legs spread wide, teeth bared. It came down on the big man from Arkansas, knocking him to the ground. The Colt was pinned on Raider's stomach. With his free hand he grabbed the cougar's throat, wrestling in the tiny rivulet, hoping that he could reach the knife in his boot.

As quickly as it had attacked, the cat went limp. Raider rolled the carcass off his body. He jumped to his feet, fanning back the hammer of the Colt. The cat twitched in a pool of its own blood. Raider had hit him with the .45 while the cougar was in the air. He felt along the animal's warm stomach to find the bullet hole in its chest.

Raider took inventory of his own wounds. He had a gash in his hand, from the cougar's teeth. Four shallow claw marks were scrawled across his burly chest. He felt the blood on his fingers, shaking his head, thinking that he would have been dead if he hadn't hit the cat with his last shot.

Raider remembered the woman and started to stagger toward the cave. The gray's dying breath stopped him. He turned back toward the horse and walked slowly to the huge carcass, hoping there was no second cat nearby. He bent over to touch the wound on the gray's neck. The blood was steaming in the cool air.

"Son of a bitch had to kill my horse."

The cougar had been efficient in his strike. Raider was angry, angry at circumstance more than the cat. The mountain lion had simply been looking for a meal. It was probably an old one taking advantage of an easy kill on a tied-up domestic animal. Raider quickly stripped the saddle and the blanket. He threw both over his shoulder and started back toward the cave.

"You're alive!" Angelica said as he pushed his way into the recess.

"Yeah, but I'm bleeding."

He threw her the horse blanket.

"You can be warm now, Angel."

"Where did this come from?"

"From our dead mount," he scowled. "Old cougar got him. Almost got me."

She wrapped her arms around him, kissing his face. Raider pushed her away and dropped the saddle. If Angelica was like other women, he thought, she would sure as hell try to bandage his wounds. He heard the ripping sounds as she started to tear wrappings from her dress.

"Where are you hurt, cowboy?"

"Left hand," he replied. "Lucky it wasn't my gun hand. Ow, careful there, lady."

Raider took a small bottle from his saddlebags.

"What are you doing?" Angelica asked.

Raider uncorked the bottle. "It's somethin' Doc give me. He said I could put it on wounds, use it for horse liniment, or drink it."

He poured some of the tincture on his chest and hand, sucking air as the pain burned through the gashes. Angelica wrapped the piece of cloth around his palm and then dabbed at the blood on his chest. Raider sat down and leaned against his saddle. If Sturgess and his men were close by, they surely heard the shots from his Colt. It might take them a while to find him, but they would have a better bearing now.

"I don't think the wounds are deep," Angelica said.

Raider lifted the bottle to his lips and drank the rest of the tincture. It burned going down, but it helped to ease the pain a little. Angelica wiped his forehead with the hem of her dress.

"You are brave, Raider. The bravest man I've ever known."

Raider laughed. Courage wasn't going to get them out of the ravine. They were going to have to walk out. And he was pretty sure that Harv Sturgess would be waiting for them when they did.

Raider's head was aching when he stirred, but the pain quickly gave way to another sensation. Angelica had unbuttoned his pants while he was asleep. Her hands worked on the growing length of his cock, stroking him as though they had awakened in the fine feather bed of a San Francisco whorehouse. He was about to protest when she lowered her mouth to him. He allowed her to continue, thinking that it might very well be his last pleasure on earth before he faced a blazing six-gun.

Angelica looked up to see his eyes staring down at her. She removed her lips and smiled, keeping her hands on his thick manhood. One time in Denver, six whores had lined up to take turns with Raider's equine member. His head was spinning with a feverish confusion.

"You think that's gonna get us out of here?" he growled.

"Shall I stop?" she replied, one eyebrow raised.

"No."

Her mouth fell on him again. Raider realized that dawn was breaking outside their cave. He had slept through the night, but he still felt exhausted. He remembered a nightmare about a mountain lion and the gray, until the pain in his hand reminded him that it wasn't a dream. Angelica's lips called him away from the dull aching.

She was quite adept at her ministrations. Raider's swelling shaft had responded before the rest of his body, but the fever was spreading to every inch of his solid frame. He reached for her breasts with his good hand. Angelica pulled her dress down over her shoulders, revealing the tight circles of her brown nipples. Raider tickled the erect bud between his fingers.

Even after sleeping under the horse blanket, after riding through the hellish night, she still smelled like a woman. Raider ran his hands down her stomach toward the dark patch of hair between her legs. When he could not reach her femininity, she pulled her body around and spread her dark thighs.

"You're a damned beautiful woman, Angel."

Her lips came off him for a second. "And you've got the biggest Johnson I've ever seen."

She went back to work immediately. Raider slowly dipped his fingers in the wet crevice between her thighs. He was searching for a certain spot where women liked to be touched. He didn't know what it was, but when you touched them there, they went a little bit crazy. Angelica was no exception. When he found the right fold of pink flesh, her body started to tremble.

"We're a pair, ain't we?" Raider said. "Somebody's waitin' out there to kill us and we're in here ready to fuck."

She laughed and came up smiling. "If we were in Phoenix, I would fix you the finest breakfast." She went down again.

When he rode the trail, through rain and dust storms, Raider thought about women like Angelica. He sustained himself with notions of feather beds and hot baths. Her mouth was a mocking reminder of the danger that awaited them at first light. Raider felt the rising stream in the length of his manhood, the force of pleasure finding its way toward her mouth.

He touched Angelica on the crown of her head but she did not come up. He exploded inside her mouth. She drank the evidence of his release. Raider's body went limp.

"I hope you aren't through," said Angelica. "I want you inside me. It's my turn for pleasure now."

Raider watched as she lifted her dress and straddled his crotch. Her soft hands, which had never known common labor, wrapped around the thickness of his manhood, guiding him toward the crest of her female prize. He wondered how long he would stay hard, but then he realized that her skills precluded any effort on his part.

Her hips, like her breasts, were full and firm. Slowly she worked his penis into her, piercing the curly wedge below her stomach. Angelica gasped, hesitating before she started her slow rise and fall. Raider marveled at the sustained hardness that seemed to have a life of its own.

"Touch my breasts," she moaned.

Raider obeyed, cupping her bosom with both his hands. He

felt her nipples tighten, even under the clumsy attempts of his bloodstained fingers. Her silky hand reached back to fondle the sack of his testicles, prompting his rigid response.

"You're growing inside me, cowboy. Don't shoot yet. Hold it there . . . let me . . . uh . . ."

Raider felt her spasms. The shiver ran through her body, culminating at her shoulders. She leaned forward on his chest until he cried out with pain. Her breasts had brushed against the claw marks from the cougar. Angelica touched his mustache with her fingertips.

"Forgive me, my loved one," she whispered. "You are bringing me so much pleasure, and I only hurt you."

"You didn't mean it."

Her hands caressed his face, tracing the lines of his rugged countenance. She ran her fingers through his coarse hair, smiling down at her lover. Slight moans emanated from her mouth, hissing sounds of delight through clenched teeth. If Harv Sturgess killed them, Raider wondered, would he go to hell for having his pleasure with Angelica so close to his death?

"I want to satisfy you again, cowboy," she whispered, nibbling on his ear. "I want your pleasure inside me."

Raider sighed. "It's up to you, lady. If you can get it out of me, it's yours."

She put her hands down on the floor of the cave, bracing herself for something. Raider watched her jiggling breasts as she began to ride him like a prize stallion. Her body seemed to be made of a supple, untiring substance. With each rotation of her hips, she flowed wetter and wetter. Raider just leaned back against the saddle, surrendering to her motion.

"Do it, cowboy. I know you can. A man like you . . . uh . . ."

She had *done it*, Raider thought, again and again, each cascading release stronger than the last. A surge of adrenaline shot through his body, erasing most of the aches and pains. He reached behind her with his good hand, cupping her meaty buttocks, rubbing the crack of her ass with his palm.

"Yes," she said softly. "You know so much about women. You are my cowboy. Oh my God . . ."

Their pleasure was accentuated by the threat of danger. Raider's breath was heavy and erratic. He strained, trying to force his second climax. But it would not come, not with her on top. He grabbed her and rolled her off him. Her back hit the moist bed of lichens.

"What are you doing?"

Raider was on his knees, gazing down at her luscious body. "I'm gonna get on top for a while."

She smiled wickedly. "You are stronger than I thought."

She spread her legs, raising her feet toward the ceiling of the cave. Raider positioned himself in the notch of her legs. He poked awkwardly, missing the mark, unable to balance himself on his good arm. Angelica knocked his hand away and guided him inside her.

A rush of hot air escaped from her lungs when he penetrated the soft folds of her vagina. The size of his manhood was no problem for her, as it had been for certain women in his past. She wrapped her legs around his waist, trapping him between her thighs. Raider started to move his hips.

"Slowly, cowboy."

"Am I hurtin' you?"

Her face contorted with a grimace of delight. "No. I just want to feel you there. I just want you to stay inside me forever. We will never leave this place."

Raider tried the slow movement. Her cunt gripped him as he rose and fell with a deliberate reserve. Finally he could no longer contain himself. He was going to complete his pleasure in his own way. Even if she didn't like it.

"Hold on, girl, I'm comin' home."

"What are you . . . yes, faster, harder . . . as hard as you . . . oh . . ."

"Hang on, woman, this is gonna be some ride."

Her ass bounced off the floor of the cave as she met each thrust. Raider was not aware of his wounds. He drove his cock in and out of her, concentrating on the tingle in his groin. As his pleasure began to rise, he steadied himself, increasing his motion for one final thrust.

"You can do it, cowboy," she groaned. "Do it inside me."

Raider grunted and released his climax. He fell on top of her, both of them quivering in the damp morning air. Their body heat warded off the cold, protecting them from the chill. Raider tried to pull out of her, but Angelica wrapped her arms around his shoulders, using her feminine strength to hold him within for a few more precious seconds.

Raider felt the reality of pain and peril coming back to him. "Ain't you had enough?"

He saw the fear in her eyes again. He brushed a lock of hair off her face and smiled. She tried to smile back, but she was hesitant. Tears began to roll out of her brown eyes.

"We can't stay here, can we, cowboy?"

Raider shook his head. Her body relaxed, allowing him to withdraw. Their pleasure was over. Once more they faced the threat of Harv Sturgess and his gang. Raider leaned back against the saddle, buttoning his pants. Angelica sat up and straightened her dress.

"What do we do now?" she asked. "Sturgess will be looking for us."

There was a strange glow in Raider's black eyes. He reached for his Colt and his Winchester. He shook his head and laughed.

"Angel, I don't feel so bad no more. You done us both a world of good."

Her brow wrinkled. "I don't know what you mean, cowboy."

"You still got that derringer I gave you?"

She nodded. The small pistol was hidden in a fold of her tattered dress. Raider took her hand and looked into her brown irises.

"Don't be scared, honey. I know we got our balls on a anvil and Harv Sturgess is the blacksmith. But we also got our guns, and I ain't never been the type to give up nothin'."

Angelica smiled "I can see that, cowboy. I can see it in your black eyes. What do you want to do?"

"Let's get the hell out of here."

They gathered up their belongings and pushed their way into the frigid Arizona morning. Raider wasn't scared or tired anymore. He just wanted a chance to face Harv Sturgess. And he didn't care if Sturgess brought along every damned gunman in the territory to back him up.

CHAPTER TWO

Doc Weatherbee dreamed of fine things. He saw himself in San Francisco, dressed in an expensive silk suit, strolling into the opera with a young woman on his arm. He heard the orchestra tuning up and then leading into the overture from *Così Fan Tutte*. But the vision began to sour quickly. The orchestra faded, and the actors' costumes began to melt right there on stage. An usher prodded Doc in the ribs, telling him that he had taken the wrong box seat. The usher's hand stirred him out of a fitful slumber, only it was not an usher at all, but the pointed boot-tip of Harv Sturgess, his captor.

"Get your ass up, Pinkerton."

There was no opera, no San Francisco, only the cold, hard ground where they had camped for the night. Doc shifted, looking up at the thin face of Harv Sturgess. Sturgess turned away and walked back toward the smell of coffee. Doc figured he would not be privy to a hot, steaming mug of the dark liquid. Sturgess would not waste it on a dead man.

With his hands still tied behind him, Doc had a rough time getting to his feet. His arms and legs were stiff from sleeping bound on the frigid earth. He was glad there was no mirror to

17

mock his disheveled appearance. Dust and grime covered the remains of his suit, and his Melton overgaiters were damaged beyond recognition. Minuscule creatures seemed to be playing Indian games in his sandy hair. He wondered if Sturgess might honor a last request for a bath and an Old Virginia cheroot.

Doc moved toward the fire where Sturgess huddled with two of his men. They had heard the shots in the night, after Little left the camp. Sturgess peered toward the mountains, trying to mark the location. With the echoes on the slopes, it was hard to tell where the shots had come from.

"I'm thinkin' it come from over yonder," said one of his henchmen.

Sturgess tipped back his Stetson. "Maybe. They were headin' that way. Due west. I don't know this area too good, though. We're gonna have to look for the trail."

"Gonna be hard on this tough ground. All rocks."

They weren't looking at Doc. He stood behind them, his hands still tied. If he could somehow get to one of the mounts, he might be able to jump into the saddle from behind. He'd have to make a running start. Raider had done it on many occasions. He started inching toward the horses.

"That's far enough, Pink-man."

Sturgess hadn't even looked around. Doc heard the chortle of a rifle lever. He turned back toward the fire and stared down the barrel of a Winchester.

"You are a most formidable opponent," Doc said.

Sturgess nodded to his man, who urged Doc toward the fire with the barrel of the rifle. Doc sat down next to Sturgess, who reached behind him. His bonds were suddenly loosened. Sturgess had cut the rope with a sharp knife.

"Give him a cup of coffee."

The tin cup burned his hands, but Doc didn't care. He sipped the steaming potion, feeling the blood as it rushed into his fingers. Sturgess was looking at him from the corners of his snaky eyes. He was up to something, Doc thought.

"You hear those shots last night, Pinkerton?"

Doc nodded.

"Where'd they come from?"

Doc lowered the coffee from his lips. "Surely you don't expect me to help you, Sturgess? I can't betray my part-ner—"

Sturgess knocked the coffee cup from his hands. "I'll tell you what you can and can't do, Pinkerton."

Sturgess stood up and looked toward the purple peaks of the mountains. The sun was bathing the slopes in warm light from the east. In the basin where they had camped, the shadows still prevailed, making the air cold. Sturgess was nervous about something. Doc decided to augment the confusion in order to increase his chances for escape.

"Raider is out there, Harv. He's waiting for you. If I were you, I'd give up while you're still alive. Don't believe for one moment that he's a helpless cowboy. Why, I've seen him—"

Sturgess wheeled around, catching Doc's face with the flat of his hand. Doc fell backward away from the fire. A trickle of blood spilled down from his lips, pooling on his chin. Doc's face flushed, and his eyes burned with anger.

"You're awfully adept at slapping men while your goons cover them with rifles," Doc said. "I suppose you learned to do that while you were learning to kidnap defenseless women."

Sturgess drew the heavy Colt from his holster. "That's enough out of you, boy. If you want to die now, keep talking."

Doc found it easier to be silent when he was staring down the bore of the Colt. Sturgess gave the order for Doc to be tied up. Thick ropes once again restricted the circulation in his limbs. Doc wondered what Sturgess would do if he faced him in a fair fight. He seemed like a man who preferred the odds stacked in his favor.

"What do you want us to do with him, Harv?" asked one of the henchmen.

"I don't know."

"He's gonna—"

"I said I don't know!" Sturgess snapped. "Leave me alone for a little while. Just leave me be!"

"Are we goin' into the mountains?" asked the other man.

Sturgess rubbed his chin. "Not now."

"I think we oughta—"

Sturgess bristled at his follower. "You ain't here to think, son. You're here to do what I tell you! Have you got that?"

The man nodded. He took Doc's arm and led him away from the fire. Sturgess kicked over the coffeepot, causing the hot liquid to extinguish the remaining circle of embers. Doc smiled to himself.

"What's so funny, Pinkerton?" asked the man with the rifle.

"Your boss seems to be out of sorts," Doc replied. "Perhaps he—"

The man put the rifle barrel in Doc's back. "Shut up and git over there by the horses."

Doc staggered over the dusty ground, thinking he might have another chance to escape. The man with the rifle came with him, however, keeping his distance as he held the Winchester on Doc. Outlaws always had a healthy respect for a Pinkerton operative. Some agents weren't human, or so the legends went. Doc knew better. His pains reminded him of his own mortality.

"Your boss isn't too happy," Doc said. "I wonder why?"

"If you're so damned smart, Pink-man, why don't you figure it out?"

Doc felt a rush of energy with the sudden realization. If he had not been so beat up, the source of Harv Sturgess's consternation would have been immediately apparent to him. In the course of the night, Little had not returned. There were only three of them by the fire. The tracker was still somewhere in the mountains. And if he had found Raider, Doc thought, the resounding echoes of gunfire might have been Little's epitaph.

Raider stole silently down the narrow stream with Angelica in his tracks. When they neared the fallen body of the cat, Angelica gasped and drew in closer to him. Raider dropped his saddle and slipped his arm around her shoulder. She was shivering in the damp air.

"He looks so sad," she whimpered.

"Think that's sad, take a gander at the gray."

Raider gestured toward the dead horse. When the air warmed up, the buzzards would be circling overhead, marking their location for anybody who wanted to find them. They had to get up high, where they could see everything. Surprise was the only thing in Raider's favor. And he would have to be damned smart to get any kind of an edge against superior numbers.

"Stay here, Angel. I'm gonna go out into the ravine and have a look-see."

"I want to come with you, cowboy. I'm afraid to stay here alone."

Raider shook his head. "You hold tight, and if you hear anything, you hightail it back to that cave, you hear?"

Her eyes were pleading as she gazed up at him. Raider kissed her for a moment. It was a tender gesture. Maybe his last if some luck didn't come his way.

"You do like I say, Angel."

"But I—"

"Say you'll do what I told you. Say it!" His teeth were clenched.

She looked down at the ground and nodded. Raider drew his Colt and started for the ravine. As he stepped over the body of the gray, he didn't even look at the cat's teeth marks in the horse's neck. He was having some damned bad luck. The kind of luck that didn't turn around so easy.

Pausing at the entrance to the crevice, Raider listened, hearing only the rushing sound of water. Maybe Sturgess had given up. Maybe he had run back to Phoenix to get his boss out of jail. Raider took a deep breath and stepped out into the ravine.

The stream was beautiful in first light, Raider thought. Blue, swirling water frothed over smooth rocks that had been washed shiny by hundreds of years of erosion. A deep pool had formed at the junction of the two streams. Raider's throat was dry. He glanced in both directions, shifting the Colt into his injured hand before he bent to drink. The cool water never reached his lips.

There was a rustling sound behind him. He looked over his shoulder to see a dark, flying shape against the sky. A glint of steel preceded the crashing weight that knocked the Colt from his hand. The pistol fell into the pool with Raider right behind it. Frigid mountain water engulfed his body.

"Come on up out of there, Pinkerton," said the man called Little. "I reckon you're finished with your bath."

Raider stood up in the knee-deep pool. The glint of steel was a bowie knife in Little's hand. Raider looked down into the water, searching for his own weapon. Little's laughter filled the hollow ravine.

"I done got the drop on you, big man. They say a big man has the edge, but looks like I'm the one with the . . ."

Raider sank back into the pool, feeling in the rocks for his Colt. When he did not find the pistol, he came up with a stone that he launched in the direction of the small man. Little side-stepped the projectile. Raider took a step toward him until he saw the Navy Colt in his scrawny hand.

"Knife and a gun," Little said. "Can't beat that, Pinkerton."

"Go to hell, Shorty."

Little thumbed back the hammer of the Navy Colt. "You talk mighty brave for a man who's about to meet his Maker."

"Do it," Raider barked. "Get it over with."

Little's rat face slacked into a frown. "Where's the woman?"

"What woman?"

"That whore. Don't lie to me, big man. If you bear false witness, St. Peter won't let you through the Pearly Gates." He looked away for a moment.

Raider started to take another step. Little urged him back. Raider's black eyes were burning. He was barely aware of the freezing water on his legs.

"What do you know about heaven, Little? You sure as hell ain't goin' there. You're one ugly little dwarf."

Little licked his lips. "The woman, Pinkerton."

Raider shrugged. "She's dead. Fell off the gray and broke her neck. She's layin' out there on the plain somewhere. I had to leave her."

"How I know you're tellin' the truth?"

Raider pointed to the sky. "Take a look when the sun's high. You'll see the buzzards over her. I didn't get time to bury her. Hell, maybe the coyotes done dragged her off."

Little grunted. "I ain't fallin' for that one, Pinkerton. If I look up at the sky, you're liable to make a move."

"Then kill me now, boy."

"I kill you, you can't lead me to the woman. I know you got her stashed back up in them mountains somewhere. Hell, I been lookin' for you all night. And you was damned surprised when I did. I knocked you into that water as big as life."

His eyes narrowed. Had he seen the shiver that ran through Raider's shoulders? Raider was starting to feel the chill. His lips were turning blue. There was no feeling in his legs.

Little gestured with the gun barrel. "You like that bath, Pinkerton? Looks like you're gettin' a mite cold to me."

Raider tried not to show it. "I'm fine, little man. Why don't you come on in here and join me?"

Little's jack-o'-lantern smile spread over his face. "Get down in the pool, big man. Go on. I'm gonna freeze it out of you. When you're cold enough, you'll tell me what I want to know."

Raider immersed himself in the icy water. His numbed hands searched for his Colt on the bottom of the pool. When he struck metal, he shifted his body to allow his good hand to close over the butt of the .45.

"Where's the woman?" Little asked.

"Dead. Like I told you. Look up in the sky. You'll see the buzzards."

Little could not resist a glance at the blue expanse overhead. When his ratty eyes turned upward, Raider brought the Colt out of the pool. He squeezed the trigger, but the cartridge did not explode. Little flinched and threw the hunting knife at him. Raider dodged the blade, thumbing back the hammer of the .45. Another dud prevented him from killing Little.

"Drop it, boy," Little cried.

Raider let the Colt fall back into the pool. Little was shaking where he stood. Staring into the bore of the pistol had rattled him. Raider wondered if he had a chance to go for the knife that had struck the wall behind him. Little probably wasn't going to give him the opportunity.

"That's all for you, Pinkerton. Tell me where you hid the woman."

"Piss on you, you weasel-faced buffalo chip. I ain't tellin' you a goddamn thing. You'd just kill me anyway."

Little extended the Navy Colt. "Then you're dead, big man. As dead as a doornail."

Raider thought about diving in either direction, but he realized that Little would get him anyway. He tried not to close his eyes, but he couldn't help it. There was something in a man that just didn't want to face death. A shot exploded, but Raider knew from the sound that it wasn't the Navy. He opened his eyes to see Little slumping to the ground. The Colt went off, but the slug struck hard rock instead of Raider's heart.

Angelica stood over the dead man, holding the derringer that Raider had given her. Both barrels of the tiny pistol smoked in the morning chill. She had shot him in the back of the head, almost at point-blank range. Angelica dropped the .32 and started to cry.

Raider came out of the pool, moving slowly with frozen limbs. "I thought I told you to stay back."

She wrapped her arms around him, bawling. For once, Raider was damned glad that women always did as they pleased. If she had obeyed him, he'd be swimming in his own blood. He touched her black hair.

"I've never killed a man before," she sobbed.

Raider grunted. "You ain't killed much of one now, lady. That little varmint never was a real man anyhow."

"May the blessed Virgin forgive me." She made the sign of the cross.

Raider pushed her away and lifted her chin. "God ain't gonna do nothin' but smile on you for killin' this bastard."

"Kiss me, cowboy."

"Not now, honey. We got to get out of here before Sturgess finds us. He heard them shots, I reckon, and he'll be comin' this way 'fore long."

"Yes, yes."

Raider went back into the pool for his Colt. He holstered the .45 and then bent down to pick up the Navy. It was an old gun, but it would have to do. And he still had his Winchester in the scabbard on his saddle. There were also two more .32 cartridges in his saddlebags. He planned on keeping the lady's weapon loaded. She was damned handy to have around.

Angelica was staring into his black eyes. "What are we going to do now?"

"I'm gonna get my rifle," Raider replied. "And then we're gonna climb."

"Climb?"

He pointed to the slopes above. "I figure ole Sturgess is gonna come in one of these ravines. When he does, I want to be up high, like a cat. I want to spring down on him from a perch. Unless you got some other ideas."

"No."

An intrepid breath escaped from Raider's lungs. As he plodded back for his rifle, he wondered why he liked his job so much. Maybe he was starting to feel better because his luck had shifted. With Little out of the way, the odds were more in his favor. He cocked the rifle, making sure it was in working order. Angelica was looking at him.

"What is it, lady?"

She looked away. "I'm not sure. I think I'm falling in love with you."

"It ain't love," Raider replied.

"What is it then?"

He glanced up at the mountain. "You just feel different about somebody when you've saved his life. It's a natural feelin'."

"Your life. Yes, you owe your life to me, cowboy."

Their eyes met again. Raider pulled the back of his hand over his mustache and then kissed her for a long time. When she drew away from him, he saw the first glimmer of hope in her brown irises.

"You must pay me back for saving your life, cowboy. When we are free, you have to return the favor."

Raider sighed. "Hell, I already rescued you from Harv Sturgess."

She nodded. "I am aware of that. And I must testify in Phoenix. But you still are in debt to me, cowboy. And when we are finished, if we are still alive, I will think of a way for you to repay me."

"I'm sure you will."

Raider took her hand and pulled her toward the slopes. He'd think about Phoenix when they were safe, when Doc was found and when Harv Sturgess was lying six feet under the dusty plain.

Doc looked up toward the mountains when he heard the gunshots. He knew that Little had found his partner, although he could only guess at the outcome. It took a pretty good man to get the drop on Raider. If the big man from Arkansas was true to form, Sturgess's tracker probably had his guts strewn all over the rocks.

Sturgess glared at Doc. "Sounds like your boy is a goner, Pink-man."

Doc tried to sit up straight. "Time will tell, my friend. Unless you're willing to go in and see for yourself."

Both of Sturgess's men were staring at him. Sturgess took

a deep breath, his hand on the butt of his Colt. He was the kind of man who didn't like surprises unless he was dealing them out.

"Get that fancy telescope that I took off the dandy," Sturgess said.

The man with the Winchester obeyed him. Doc watched as Sturgess lifted the spyglass to his beady eye. He had taken the glass from Doc's wagon. Doc was glad that Sturgess hadn't found some of the other weapons in the Studebaker. He was dangerous enough without them.

"See anythin', Harv?"

Sturgess kept watching the mountainside. He was waiting for his man to come out of the foothills. Several minutes passed and there was still no Little. Doc grew hopeful that Raider had prevailed.

"Damn that Little," Sturgess said. "Where the hell is he?"

Doc tried not to smile. Sturgess looked back at him and scowled. At least he wouldn't kill him until he was sure the girl had been taken. Sturgess handed the telescope to the man with the Winchester.

"Keep a lookout until I say different."

The man lifted the glass to his eye. Sturgess hovered over Doc, who sat cross-legged on the ground. He grabbed Doc's lapels and pulled the gentleman Pinkerton to his feet.

"If my man is dead, neither one of you is gettin' out of here alive," Sturgess growled. "And before you die, you'll pray to God that I—"

"Harv. Come here."

Sturgess released Doc and spun around. The man with the Winchester had spotted something. Sturgess grabbed the glass and peered toward the purplish slopes. He spotted two insectlike figures climbing onto a rocky ledge.

"It's the Pinkerton," Sturgess said. "And he's got the woman."

"How we gonna get him down?" asked the man with the rifle. "He could hold off an army up there."

Sturgess shook his head. "He ain't got enough ammo. Besides, I think I got a plan. See those hills below the ledge. Let's ride for them, pronto."

The man with the Winchester turned toward Doc. "What are we gonna do with the dandy, Harv?"

"Put him on a horse and drag him along. We're gonna need him."

Sturgess's pair of henchmen jostled Doc onto the back of the black gelding. As they rode hard for the foothills, Doc had a disquieting thought. Raider was alone against three of them. Usually it was through teamwork that they solved a predicament. Sturgess might be too clever. Doc wasn't sure if his partner was smart enough to deal with such a resourceful outlaw by himself.

Raider watched from the ledge as the four horses drove for the foothills. Angelica stood beside him, her brown eyes trained on the danger below. Doc's pearl-gray derby bobbed in the brightness of the eastern sun. His partner was alive at least.

"We can't stay here," Angelica said.

Raider took off his Stetson and wiped his brow. "Where else we gonna go? If Sturgess tries to come up here, I can pick him off with the rifle. If we go down, he'll catch us for certain."

Angelica frowned. "Time is his ally. We have no food or water. He can wait below for us."

"Maybe," Raider replied. "But he has somethin' more complicated in mind, otherwise he would wait out there on the plain. He's comin' in here for a reason. And I think I know what it is."

Sturgess's party disappeared behind the foothills. Raider marked the general direction and kept his eyes trained on the rise. How long would it be before Sturgess reared his ugly head? The air was suddenly hot and stifling, making the wait that much more unbearable.

Angelica was gazing down into the basin below. "Perhaps I should give myself up in exchange for your lives."

Raider laughed sarcastically. "That don't make much sense, lady. Sturgess wouldn't let us go."

"If I—"

"Put a cork in it. Just keep your eyes open."

They watched for a long time before they saw the movement in the notch between the mountain and the foothills. Raider caught glimpses of the black suit worn by Sturgess. He seemed to have another man with him, both of them moving like snakes between the rocks. Where was Doc and the other man?

"Can't you shoot them?" asked Angelica.

Raider shook his head. "Not from here. They're out of range. I couldn't even hit them with a buffalo gun. What the hell are they up to?"

Raider peered down the rocky slope into the notch. There were hundreds of rocks and boulders between them and Sturgess. He could wind his way up with no problem and Raider would never see him coming. A harsh cry rolled through the boulders, piercing the hot air.

"Pinkerton! Look down. Look at the hills!"

Raider gazed straight into the sun. Perched atop one of the foothills, high on a craggy rock formation, stood Doc and another man. With the glare it was hard to see them, but Raider was pretty sure the man held a rifle in his hands. Sturgess, who crouched below in the notch, dispelled all doubt.

"My man's got a Winchester on your partner, big man. If you don't send down the girl, he's gonna blow off the top of his head."

"Son of a bitch," Raider grumbled under his breath. Then he shouted: "Sturgess! How do I know he's my partner? You could have one of your own men dressed up in Doc's clothes!"

"Answer your partner, Weatherbee!"

Doc's unmistakable voice rolled over the notch. "Don't do it, Raider. Don't give her up. . . ."

Doc's figure buckled, as if someone had hit him in the stomach. Raider strained his black eyes, searching for Sturgess below in the rocks. If he could get off a lucky shot, maybe a richochet . . . Had his chances really come down to a desperate maneuver?

Angelica stood up with a small rock in her hand. She cursed and launched it down the slope. Raider's eyes opened wide.

"Lady, I think you got the right idea."

Angelica looked at him. "What do you mean?"

"What'll it be, Pinkerton?" cried Sturgess.

"Give me time to think," Raider called.

"You got two minutes, boy!"

"That's about all the time I'm gonna need," Raider replied to himself.

Angelica watched as the big man searched for something

on the ledge. Raider was hefting rocks one at a time, like he was weighing them. She wondered if he had lost his mind.

"What are you doing, cowboy?"

Raider tried to lift a boulder that wouldn't budge. "I'm gonna make it rain, Angel."

"Rain?"

"Help me, woman. Here, get on this side."

Together they lifted the boulder, carrying it to the edge of the overhang. Raider hesitated, peering down as if he were taking aim. The rock was becoming too heavy for Angelica. She felt her sweaty hands slipping.

"I can't hold it."

"Hush up," Raider replied. Then he shouted to Sturgess: "Okay, Harv, you win. Stay right where you are and I'll bring her down. You got to promise you won't shoot us."

"I promise," came the reply.

Raider saw the corner of a hat brim sticking out behind a rock. He tossed the boulder over the edge, watching as it crashed into the stones and boulders below. As the heavy rock fell, it loosened other stony debris. A rumbling filled the air as the rockslide began.

"It's rainin'," Raider said. "Rainin' rocks on Harv Sturgess. I just hope he brought along his slicker."

A ton of stone showered down on the notch, crashing with a burst of dust and thunder. Raider waited until the dust had cleared, and then he started down the mountainside with Angelica behind him. He wished there was some way to get in touch with Allan Pinkerton, to tell his boss that he had finished a day's work—the hard way.

When the rocks began to fall from the mountain, the man with the Winchester turned his face away from Doc. Doc seized the moment, dropping to his buttocks, kicking out his legs as he tumbled. He caught the man's knees, pushing him off the hill to his death plunge. The man's cries were muffled by Raider's noisy destruction. Doc struggled to his feet, sadly aware that the Winchester had fallen with his captor.

Doc worked at the rope bonds until his hands were free. Then he gazed down the hill toward the notch where Sturgess had been. He waited until he saw the black figure running away from the slide. The other man had not been as lucky. Only Sturgess had escaped.

Doc had a slow time going down the hill. When he was on level ground, he found the horses and mounted up, riding in the direction Sturgess had run in. Doc wondered if Raider had seen the man's timely exit.

Doc spurred a chestnut mare toward the mountains, riding as hard as the terrain would allow. He slowed when he neared the fallen rocks. A bloody arm, the remains of Sturgess's gang, protruded from the debris. How had the man in the gambler's suit gotten out of there?

"Weatherbee!"

Doc peered up to see Raider standing on a boulder. The woman was behind him. Doc realized he didn't have a weapon. There was no rifle in the scabbard on the chestnut.

"Throw me your Winchester," Doc called.

"What for?" Raider replied. "Can't you see what I done? I give ole Sturgess a headache."

"Sturgess got out. I saw him from the hill."

"How the hell—"

"He's slippery," Doc cried. "The rifle."

Raider put the Winchester in the air. Doc caught it and turned the chestnut away from the rubble. Raider called after him as he chased Sturgess's trail.

"I'll circle around the other way, Doc."

But he only cried out into a cloud of dust.

Doc abandoned the chestnut when the terrain became too rocky. Sturgess had run into an area of large boulders and craggy ledges. There were hundreds of nooks and crannies where he might lay low, waiting with his Colt to ambush anyone who followed his trail. Doc surveyed the mountainside, listening for the tell tale scuffling of a man climbing the slopes.

Sturgess was halfway up the incline, making for the peak. Doc saw the black Stetson first. He watched for a time to make sure it was Sturgess. When he was certain, he started up the hill after him.

Doc did not make any effort to conceal himself. He went straight up as fast as he could climb, keeping the Winchester ready. When Sturgess saw him, he emptied his Colt, sending slugs into the rocks around Doc's feet. The Winchester answered, pinning Sturgess to the side of the mountain.

Doc cried out angrily, remembering the discomfort caused him by the man in the gambler's suit. "Give it up, Sturgess. You're a dead man if you don't."

"Come and get me, Pinkerton!"

Doc did just that. He kept climbing, stopping to fire on Sturgess whenever he tried to move. Doc emerged on a flat ledge below the man in black. He had a clear shot and drew a bead with the rifle.

"Are you coming down, Sturgess? Or do I have to kill you?"

Sturgess was trying to reload the Colt. Doc fired off a round, knocking the pistol from his hand. Sturgess trembled on the rocks, looking down at Doc like an animal in the gates of a slaughterhouse.

"Don't shoot, Weatherbee! In the name of God, don't shoot!"

Doc levered the Winchester. "I ought to take you right now, Sturgess. I've a good mind to save the territorial government the effort of hanging you. I'd be doing everyone a favor."

Another howling cry rolled over the mountainside. Doc looked up to see Raider standing above them. He had come around on the backside of the slopes. He waved to his partner.

"We got him, Doc. Let him come up or down. He ain't going anywhere."

Doc held the Winchester to his shoulder. "He was going to kill us, Raider. Why shouldn't we return the favor?"

Sturgess's voice was a weak whimper. "No, Weatherbee. Please. Don't kill me. I . . . no . . . ."

"Listen to him," Doc cried. "When the boot is on the other foot, he's as meek as a lamb. I ought to—"

"That ain't you," Raider called back. "You can't kill him, Doc. You ain't the kind to kill a man in cold blood. I don't care if he did ruin your suit and keep you hog-tied."

Doc bristled. "Why can't I kill him? He's probably left a trail of dead men all over this country."

"How you gonna explain it to Pinkerton?" Raider cried. "I can't lie for you, Doc. Not if you go against everything we stand for."

Doc exhaled and lowered the Winchester. Raider was right. If Sturgess could be taken alive, he had to do it—no matter how much the man needed killing. Doc would not allow himself to be so unprofessional.

"Come down, Sturgess," he cried. "We're taking you back to Phoenix to stand trial with the others."

Sturgess started to move, but not toward Doc. He scrambled on the incline, moving straight toward Raider. Doc leaned back and watched him. He would never get past the big man from Arkansas.

"The rat is coming your way."

"I got him," Raider replied.

Sturgess lifted himself onto a narrow ledge in front of a deep cave. He looked down at Doc, shaking his fist. His hateful voice echoed through the hollows of the range.

"Try to get me down if you can, Pinkerton. I'll never . . . what . . . my God, I . . ."

Raider had the best vantage point from above. He saw the blur of brown fur as the cougar leapt from the recesses of the cave. The animal caught Sturgess by the neck and shook him like a child's straw doll. Before Raider could get off a shot, Sturgess tumbled down the slope toward an abrupt splattering on the point of a boulder.

Doc and Raider were stunned. The big man stood against the sun, holding the Winchester on his hip. Doc looked up and shrugged his shoulders. Raider was shaking his head.

"Musta been the mate of that cougar that got my gray."

The cat's eyes rolled up at him, offering a brief scowl before the rippling fur skulked back into the cave. Probably, Raider thought, it was a female with a litter of young crying in the dark. She was waiting for her mate to bring back meat for the cubs. Sturgess would have been alive if he hadn't climbed that extra ten feet to the ledge.

"Meet you down below," Raider called. "Ain't no need to pick up what's left."

When they were standing together, Doc saw that Raider had his arm around the woman's shoulder. He dusted off his derby and bowed to Angelica. She did not smile. They were all tired as hell.

"Nature has a way of taking care of men like Harv Sturgess," Doc offered.

"I thought you was gonna take care of him there for a

minute," Raider replied. "I ain't never seen you so mad, Doc."

"I'm fine now." His voice was hollow.

"Come on," Raider said. "Let's get the hell out of here."

"There are some men in Phoenix who'll be very surprised to see us," Doc replied. "Very surprised."

A dry smirk drew across Raider's lips. "That's a shame, Doc. A cryin' damn shame."

They were silent again as they began to round up the horses.

CHAPTER THREE

The silhouetted structures of Phoenix rose up abruptly out of the plain, shaded and colored by the purple morning sky to the east. The air smelled of fresh rain, a brief shower that surrendered to the coming heat of day. Doc Weatherbee stretched in the seat of the Studebaker wagon, trying to ease the stiffness that came with riding all night. He glanced over at his partner, who dozed in the saddle of the chestnut mare. Raider's ability to fall asleep had amazed Doc since they were forced to work as a team by Allan Pinkerton. The big man could nap through an Indian attack.

"Raider!"

No response from under the brim of the Stetson. Doc picked up his buggy whip and snapped it in front of Raider's face. Raider cried out and brought up his Peacemaker.

"What the hell are you doin', Doc?"

Doc nodded toward Phoenix in the distance. Raider rubbed his eyes and sat up straight in the saddle. It was good to see civilization for a change. He holstered his weapon and rode along next to the Studebaker.

"Thought we'd never get here," Raider said. "Where's the woman?"

"Sleeping in back of the wagon," Doc replied. "She's as tired as we are."

They had spent the better part of the previous day rounding up horses and retrieving Doc's wagon from Harv Sturgess's camp. They agreed on riding straight through the night, since the sky was clear and the North Star bright. Phoenix was closer than Raider had figured. He had only been in the saddle for twelve hours, when he had estimated a whole day of riding time.

The sight of Phoenix on the horizon gave Raider a burst of energy. He was thinking of a bathhouse, a warm bed, country-fried steak, and another session with a willing female. He was getting ready to spur the chestnut when Doc reined his beloved mule, Judith.

Raider halted the chestnut and scowled at his partner. "You're pickin' a fine time to stop."

Doc's hand rested on his chin. He tipped back the soiled derby and peered into the distance. Raider had seen the look countless times. Doc was figuring something, a new slant, an angle that a normal man might miss. Doc's figuring made Raider nervous sometimes, but it was better to have him cog-itating—a lot of times it saved their lives.

"What's on your mind, Weatherbee?"

"Our precious cargo," Doc replied.

"I ain't followin' you." Raider looked back toward the town.

"Raider, do you recall the name of the man who's imprisoned? The man who will remain incarcerated with Angelica's testimony?"

Raider took off his Stetson. "Hell, Doc, they got three of 'em locked up in there."

"There's only one of them who has any power, however—Long."

Raider gestured toward the back of the Studebaker. "Is that the one who Angel's gonna hang?"

Doc nodded. "And Mr. Long is not pleased. Until she agreed to testify, he was quite powerful in these parts. Now he's in jail without bond. He can only get out if Angelica does not appear in court."

Raider shrugged. "Tell me somethin' I don't know, Doc."

"Try this," Doc replied. "If Long was willing to hire Sturgess to take Angelica away, then what prevents him from hiring someone to make sure we don't bring her back into town?"

"Yeah, I see what you're gettin' at."

Raider thought about everything they had been through to make sure Angelica Maria Del Gado returned to Phoenix. They had come too far to get bushwhacked at the last minute. Doc was right as usual.

Raider slipped on his hat. "What are we gonna do about it?"

Doc turned toward his partner. "What do you suggest?"

Raider drew the rifle from the scabbard on the chestnut's saddle. He flipped the Winchester in his hand, levering a round into the chamber as it spun. He laughed a little and pointed toward Phoenix with the rifle barrel.

"I say we take her right down goddamn Main Street, Doc. If anybody tries to stop us, we shoot their ass off."

Doc was skeptical. "Throw caution to the wind, as it were. I don't agree. I say we slip in quietly, down a back alley."

Raider sighed. "Shit, sneakin' around like a couple of criminals. That ain't our style."

"No, but caution is."

"Okay," Raider said. "How about this? You sneak in, and I'll ride right down Main Street. That way we cover both sides of the river."

Doc thought about it for a moment before he agreed. "I'll go ahead of you, then. Give me at least a half hour. You'll be able to watch me. When my wagon is out of sight, you should be able to catch up easily."

"I knowed you'd find a way to keep me out of town as long as possible."

Doc looked sternly at his partner. "Raider, we may have to testify to the kidnapping charges. I certainly hope you don't jeopardize our credibility as witnesses."

"What?"

"Don't get into any trouble in Phoenix!"

"Hell, Doc, you oughta know better than that."

Doc surely did.

Raider was tired of waiting after ten minutes had passed. He pulled down the brim of his black Stetson and spurred the chestnut mare. There was a corral on the edge of town. He could stable the chestnut and secure the general area for Doc's arrival. Doc would probably bring the wagon in from the north, down an alley that would let him stop behind the hotel. He could slip Angelica in the back way and nobody would ever see them.

The corral was still in place, but three new fixtures had been added. Against the wooden rails leaned a trio of armed men. Their guns were slung low, holsters tied above the knee— the look of hired shootists. Raider slowed the mare when he saw them. The Winchester came out of the scabbard to rest on his left thigh. Right hand over the Colt.

Raider swung his legs off the saddle and crouched low for a moment. The three of them had seen him. Two of them moved left, hands full of Colt iron. Raider lifted the rifle to his shoulder. The Winchester barked twice and the men fell, clutching holes in their chests. Raider looked toward the corral. The third man had disappeared.

Raider called into the cool morning air, ripe with burnt powder, "You gonna try me, boy?"

No reply. He rattled the lever of the Winchester. The man had to be hiding behind the water trough. Raider put two rounds into the wooden planks.

"Son of a biscuit-eater," cried the third man. "You done got me all wet!"

"Hightail it, boy, or you're gonna get what I gave your partners."

Raider started to swing left as the man replied, "Why'd you take out my men?"

Raider stopped and crouched again. "They was drawin' down as soon as they seen me. You're Long's hired men. Come to stop us from deliverin' that girl. Ain't you?"

"So you're the Pinkerton."

Raider moved again, watching the trough between the slats of the corral.

"No wonder you took them out so quick. That's far enough, partner. I know you're coming around on the rail. One more step and I'll have you—"

A pistol chattered, kicking up splinters in front of Raider. He launched his own volley with the Winchester. The water trough was draining on all sides.

Raider peeked over the top of the fence. "Who the hell are you, boy?"

"Call me Johnny Frisco."

Raider tipped back his Stetson. "The California Kid?"

"I been called that."

"Long must be payin' better than day wages."

The man behind the trough was silent. Raider wondered if the local law authorities had heard the shooting. The marshal was doing his best to keep men like the California Kid out of Phoenix. No wonder he wanted to hang Long and his compatriots.

"Pinkerton! Looks like we got ourselves a standoff."

"I ain't followin' you, Johnny."

"You can't just let me walk out of here, can you, Pinkerton?"

Raider chortled. "No, I can't, Johnny."

"I don't suppose you want to face me square."

Raider thought about it. He had shot it out with some pretty tough men in his day, but the California Kid had a reputation for being quick and accurate. On the other hand, he was just another damned punk who had gotten too big for his britches.

"I'll face you, son," Raider said, his voice colder than the break of day. "Course, you can always give up and come along quiet-like."

"No prison for me," replied Johnny Frisco.

"Hell, if we could get you back to California, they'd probably hang you."

"That they would, Pinkerton. That they would. How you want to do it?"

Raider tossed the Winchester toward the trough. "That was my rifle hittin' the ground. I'm comin' up on a three count, hot iron ready. You come up the same way."

Raider counted to three and stood up. Johnny Frisco's pistol erupted first. Raider felt a stinging pain in his gun hand. His Colt was lying on the ground. Johnny Frisco broke into a run, heading for town.

Raider rolled over the fence and jumped on the Winchester. He came up and put the bead in the middle of Johnny Frisco's back. "Stop it, boy!"

The California Kid wheeled on the balls of his feet, pointing a large-caliber Remington at Raider's head. Raider had to fire. A patch of red liquid flowed instantly out of Johnny Frisco's chest. He crumpled into the street.

Raider walked slowly toward the body. The last charge of life-energy was flowing out of the California Kid. He looked up at Raider with glassy eyes.

"Got me, Pink . . . uh . . ."

"Why didn't you shoot me back there, Johnny? You had me cold."

His voice was a death chortle. "Not payin' me enough to kill a Pinkerton. Long . . . cheap bas . . ."

He was gone. Not too bright a kid, Raider thought. But he had been damned fast on the draw. Too fast. Raider looked at the scratch on his gun hand. There might be a bruise but nothing that would hurt for more than a week. Doc would want to fix it up, probably. Raider wondered if he was getting too old to face down ambitious youths with blood in their eyes.

"Hold it right there, mister."

The voice had come from behind him. Raider looked over his shoulder into the twin barrels of a scattergun. The marshal, Asa Culp, stared down at the big man. Culp lowered the shotgun when he saw Raider's face.

"You!" the marshal cried. "When did you come in?"

Raider stood up and turned away from the body. "Just now, marshal. My partner's bringin' the girl from the north. I come in this way to see what they might have waitin' for us."

The marshal, a slender, neat, sometimes ineffective man, moved over the remains of the California Kid. "I been tryin' to find a reason to run him out of town. Looks like you saved me the trouble, Mr. Raider."

"You ought to try a little more firepower and a little less talk," Raider replied. "This kind don't understand law books."

Culp cast disapproving gray eyes on Raider. "I obey the letter of the law, sir. You'd do well to follow the same in this town."

Raider gestured toward the corpse. "Justifiable homicide, marshal. You think the town would pay to have them buried?"

"You killed these men because they shot at you?"

Raider nodded. "I thought that was clear, marshal. Unless you want to press charges against me."

"No. No, I couldn't do that."

"Then if you'll excuse me, I'm gonna go see if my partner is safe and sound. He's got the girl with him, too."

The marshal rested the stock of the scattergun under his arm. "I'll come along, Mr. Raider. And don't take no offense. I know you was doin' what you had to do. I just ain't happy about killin' in my town, justifiable or otherwise. The town council is . . ."

Both of them looked toward the north side of town. Gunshots echoed through the silent city streets. Raider broke into a run. The marshal was right behind him. If Culp wasn't happy about killing, he stood to be a whole lot sadder before he even had his breakfast.

When the two men opened fire on Doc Weatherbee, he dived out of the wagon seat, splashing in a puddle from the brief rain. He shouted the verbal command for Judith to halt and then rolled beneath the wagon. Rifle slugs pelted the street all around him. He reached into his coat pocket for his .38 Diamondback. A man rushed him from the shadows, prompting Doc to fire. The bullet caught the man between the eyes. He staggered backward and flopped in the street.

Judith held her position beautifully. Doc felt the wagon jostling as the woman moved above him. When she stuck out her head from the back of the wagon, the rifles chattered again. Doc reached up and pulled her down to the ground. Angelica rolled underneath the Studebaker, sliding next to Doc.

"Have they gone crazy, Doctor?"

Doc was reloading his Diamondback. "I'm not a real physician, Miss Del Gado. I do sometimes pose as an apothecary."

The rifles were persistent, ripping into the wagon. There was dynamite in one of the compartments above them. A stray slug might send them all to hell. Doc looked out, wondering if he could make a run with the woman.

"What will we do?" Angelica asked.

A voice mocked them from above. "Give up the girl, Weatherbee. Give her up or you'll never see your Pinkerton boss again."

Doc did not reply. He was waiting for Raider. He hoped he wouldn't have to wait very long.

• • •

Raider moved through the alley, clinging tightly to the damp stucco wall. The marshal moved on the other side, holding his scattergun in hand. They heard the rifles making their music. Raider could see the wagon, but he didn't see Doc. He looked over at the marshal and pointed upward.

The marshal nodded and kept moving forward. When the bushwhackers fired again, Raider saw the mud kick up next to the wagon. He also saw the dead man in the street. Doc had taken one himself.

Both assassins were hidden above, one of them on the roof and the other on an old Spanish-style balcony. Raider marked the man on the roof. It was an easy shot. The man didn't even see him. Raider gestured to the marshal. Culp nodded, telling Raider to take the man on the roof.

Raider sighted in, feeling a little bad about shooting a man who wasn't even looking at him. He squeezed the trigger and the sniper tumbled down into the alley, crashing with a meaty thud. A second rifle exploded. The stucco next to Raider's head was shattered into dust. The man from the balcony had fired on him.

As Raider dived for the ground the scattergun went off. The man on the balcony staggered, holding his groin. Culp had shot him right through the balcony floor. The man fell into the alley, twitching and screaming.

"Better get him to the doctor," the marshal said.

Raider was walking toward his partner and the woman. "You get him to a doctor, Marshal. I'm gonna make sure my partner's still alive."

The man on the ground breathed his last, freeing the marshal from his duty. He walked behind Raider. Doc and Angelica were crawling out from under the Studebaker.

Culp smiled and shook Doc's hand. "Mr. Weatherbee, I can't tell you how happy this makes me."

Doc raised his hand. "Save your accolades, Marshal. We are extremely tired and require the immediate comfort of your hotel. I trust the suites are reserved."

Culp tipped his hat. "Everything is arranged. I didn't expect you this soon, but you've come back at the right time. Judge Lutrall is due tomorrow. We can try Long and the other two."

Raider frowned at the marshal. "Are me and Doc gonna have to testify?"

Culp nodded. "By the way, Weatherbee, this telegram came for you while you were gone."

Culp took the message from his pocket and extended it toward Doc. Raider snatched the telegram out of the marshal's hand. He wasn't ready for bad news.

Doc was in no mood to play games. "Give me that cable at once," he said.

Raider grimaced. "You know what this means, Doc? Another mission."

Doc was holding his pistol. "I've shot one man today, Raider. Would you like to be the second?"

Culp's eyes were wide. He wondered if Doc was kidding. Raider didn't seem to be taking any chances. He turned the message over to his partner. Doc unfolded the paper and read carefully.

Raider put his arm around Angelica's shoulder. She moved in closer to him. Doc looked up at them with raised eyebrows.

"Somethin' wrong, Mr. Weatherbee?" the marshal asked.

"No," Doc replied. "It just says here that we are to stay in Phoenix until this present business is finished. Then we are supposed to be in St. Louis no later than the fifteenth of next month."

Raider grimaced. "St. Louis? Hell, we'll never make it."

Doc shrugged. "I don't know. Today is only the twenty-seventh. With the judge in town we should be able to give our testimony and then leave for Missouri in time to make it."

"Does it say why we're s'posed to go there?" Raider asked.

"No. Just the directive from the home office. No explanations."

Angelica cleared her throat. "Gentlemen, I must excuse myself. If the marshal will see me to my room..."

Culp smiled. "Why, of course, Miss Del Gado."

"Hey," Raider said, "maybe I ought to..."

Doc shook his head. "Let her go, Raider."

"But..."

"I know, you want to take advantage of her helplessness."

"No, Doc, it ain't like that."

The marshal ushered Raider's woman into the hotel, through

the back entrance. Angelica turned before she went in and blew a kiss to Raider.

The big man stood up a little taller. "She likes me, Doc."

Doc took Judith's harness in hand. "Somehow I'm not surprised."

"Don't be runnin' down Angel," Raider said with a scowl. "Hell, she saved my carcass out there in that ravine."

They started walking toward the livery. Doc fished in his pocket for a cigar. He had one broken stub and a single sulphur match. It was enough. Raider gagged on the smoke.

"Sorry," Doc said. "Raider, our testimony is important in this trial. Please don't do anything that might hurt our credibility."

The big man bristled. "Don't worry, Doc. I'll act like a ole lady. Just like you."

Doc puffed on the stogie. "I'm too tired to banter, Raider. Just make sure you are in court tomorrow, sober and coherent."

Raider tipped his hat and turned back toward the hotel. He didn't have any intention of staying away from Angelica Maria Del Gado. If there was any way to get to her before the trial, Raider would find it.

"Let me in, Angel. It's cold out here in the hall."

Raider had bribed the deputy who was guarding Angelica's room. He had a half hour. Her perfume seeped through the door. She was standing on the other side, probably clad in some flimsy silk nightgown. Raider remembered her supple body from the cave. And the things she had done to him.

His voice was pleading. "Honey, let me in. We won't take long. I just want to see you."

Her indecisive voice was barely audible. "I want you, cowboy, but..."

"Just open the door, Angel."

"The trial... I must sleep. It would be bad luck for us tonight. After I testify, my Raider. I will want you then even more."

Raider snorted and stomped his foot a little. The deputy marshal, a young bronc, was grinning. Raider had to save some face. He let his pride get the better of him.

"Let me in now, damn it, woman!"

No reply from the other side of the door.

Raider stepped back and straightened his body. "Okay, lady. That's it. You can't play with me like this. You don't want me now, then don't expect me to be around after the trial."

He waited, but she didn't open the door. Raider stomped out, shaking his head at the deputy marshal. The young kid was smiling.

"Guess you told her," said the deputy.

"Yeah," Raider grumbled. "I guess I did."

The trial was over in two days, largely due to the courtroom manner of Judge Jefferson Lutrall. In his ceremonious black robes, Lutrall cut a menacing, all-powerful figure that demanded total decorum and respect for procedure. Both sides unfolded their cases, the district prosecutor first, followed by the defendant's lawyer.

Angelica's testimony counted for nearly all the prosecution's evidence. She linked the defendant to several illegal bribes and transactions, including two that were also backed up by paper documentation. The defense attempted to cast aspersions on Angelica's character, alluding to her bed-sharing with the defendant. Judge Lutrall intervened on Angelica's behalf, sustaining the objection by the prosecutor.

Doc and Raider were never called as witnesses. They had to remain in Phoenix in case the prosecutor decided to press charges for kidnapping and conspiracy. They were the ace in the hole if the jury brought back a verdict of not guilty.

"Looks like they're tryin' to get old Long dead cold," Raider remarked to Doc as the jury left for deliberation.

Doc nodded, twirling his new derby in his hands. "I wonder how long the jury will take to—"

"God Almighty."

The jury was coming back into the courtroom. They hadn't even spent five minutes voting on the verdict. The judge was still in the pulpit. He pushed down the wire-rimmed spectacles on his nose and peered toward the jury foreman.

"Have you reached a verdict?"

The foreman stood up. "Yes, we have, judge."

"Will Mr. Long rise, along with the other two defendants. Foreman, read the verdict."

Guilty of all charges. A light stirring in the courtroom. Everyone had suspected it. The judge dismissed the jury and looked down at the three defendants. Raider thought he was witnessing a Last Judgment. Lutrall's eyes were alive and burning.

"They've found you all guilty, Mr. Long. I'm goin' to pass sentence on you. Ordinarily, I'd wait a spell, let you sit in the cell and think about the things you done. But I want to deal with you different than I done other men, seein's how you done so much wrong. Do you have anythin' to say before I sentence you?"

Long's weasel face was a red smirk. "Don't worry, Judge. I won't be in jail long. I've got friends around here. No jail can hold me."

The judge nodded. "I'm tendin' to agree, Mr. Long. Your smugness and your lack of repentance leads me to believe that you have no respect for the law. Therefore, since you have been found guilty of a number of charges, and since the people have ruled so decisively against you, as the presiding representative of the territorial court, I sentence you and your conspirators to hang by the neck until you are dead. Sentence to be carried out immediately."

The courtroom was buzzing. The gallery was just short of cheering. Long had almost been railroaded. Of course, he had done all the things the jury had found him guilty of, so there was no reason to feel bad for him.

"Boy," Raider said. "I hope I never have to face that damned Lutrall."

Doc laughed. "Yes, a ruffian like you would probably be put in front of a firing squad."

Raider started looking for Angelica. A bailiff was escorting her out of the courtroom. Doc saw the look in his black eyes.

"She is rather beautiful," he said.

"I can do better right here in Phoenix," Raider replied. "Remember Dorie? The one you stole from me that time."

Doc torched the end of a cheroot. "It doesn't matter. We have to leave for St. Louis immediately. Remember the directive of the home office."

"Hell, Doc, we got a little extra time now. Why can't we enjoy it?"

"Even if we travel by train it will still take us several days," Doc replied. "You can sow your wild oats in St. Louis."

"Aw, you know I don't cotton to them city women. They always feel kinda slippery. Besides, even if we do go by train, we can't leave until tomorrow afternoon."

"How do you know that?"

Raider grinned. "I knew you was gonna pull this train stuff on me, so I checked with the station. The way I figure it, I got me about twenty-four hours of free time. You too, Doc."

Doc started out of the empty courtroom with Raider behind him. When they emerged on the wooden sidewalk, Doc flipped the new derby on his head. Raider put on his Stetson.

"You know, Doc, I feel kinda good about all this."

Doc took a deep breath. "Well, this territory will be short three more scoundrels this time tomorrow. I suppose we can take some of the credit."

Raider clapped Doc on the shoulder. "Well, Weatherbee, I'm gonna go see if I can find me some sticky stuff."

"You have twenty-four hours," Doc replied. "The train leaves tomorrow at three o'clock. Don't be late."

"Nooo, uh-huh, Doc."

Raider tromped off down the sidewalk, grinning like a possum. His thoughts had already turned to a little woman named Dorie and the house she sported on the outskirts of town.

Miss Dorie Collins stood in front of Raider's bed, unfolding the blue satin robe that covered her buxom frame. Her large breasts were pushed up by the restrictive undergarment that she wore beneath the robe. Raider felt himself rising under the sheets.

The robe fell from Miss Dorie's shoulders. "Sorry I took so long, Raider. I was settlin' a debt with an old cowboy friend."

"Did he owe you, or you owe him?"

Dorie smiled. "You're lookin' fit as a fiddle. Why don't I climb into bed and lick that mustache of yours?"

Raider pointed at the corset. "Take off the hardware first. I don't like pointy things in the sack."

"Looks like you got a pointy thing under that sheet," Dorie replied.

The corset fell on top of the robe. Her body jiggled freely. Raider liked big women. They seemed to him to have a better disposition. Skinny girls were too vain sometimes. Raider threw back the sheet. Dorie's thick lips stretched into a smile.

"Ready as ever."

"And all for you," Raider replied.

Dorie never got it. The door flew open behind her. Raider reached for his gun on the nightstand, expecting to whack down a crazed cowboy who had drunk too much tequila. Instead, he aimed the Colt at a lovely dark-haired woman in a lacy white dress.

"Angel! How the hell did you—"

Dorie didn't take kindly to another female in her bedroom. She charged Angelica, holding out her claws. Angelica side-stepped her and pulled the .32 derringer from her purse. She leveled it at Dorie, who stopped dead in her tracks. Angelica's eyes were flaring.

"Tell her to leave, Raider," she said.

Dorie grabbed the blue satin robe and pulled it around her. "She can't tell me to leave. This is my house."

Angelica took a deep breath. "Very well, if she will not leave, then Raider will come with me. Is that agreeable?"

"I never should have give you that gun," Raider said.

"I saved your life, cowboy," Angelica replied. "Now it is time for you to repay me."

Raider climbed off the bed and stepped into his pants. Angelica looked away for a moment, allowing Dorie to launch another attack. She grabbed Angelica's dark hair and spun her around the room. The derringer went off, but luckily no one was hit. Raider pulled on his boots and grabbed both of the women.

"You two wildcats bring in your claws."

If he had let them go, Angelica would have prevailed, he thought. She was flaming mad—that Spanish streak in her. Raider had to admire a woman who would fight for him. He held her at arm's length while he spoke to Dorie.

"She's right, Dorie, she did save my life. Now I've got to settle up with her. You understand?"

Dorie was practically spitting as she ordered them out. "I never want to see your face in my house again, Raider. Do you understand?"

The big man from Arkansas made a quick escape with Angelica behind him. A buggy was waiting outside the cathouse. Raider helped her into the seat and climbed in beside her. Angelica's head was high. She was proud of her victory.

"Don't look so high and mighty," Raider said as he took the reins of the buggy. "I won't never be able to go back there. Leastways not for a year or so."

Angelica pouted. "How can you spend the night with a woman like that?"

"Hell, if you hadn't turned me down that night in the hotel . . . I mean, I figured you didn't want anything else to do with me. How the devil did you find me here anyway?"

"Your partner."

"It figures."

Raider shook the reins and started back toward town. As they grew closer to the hotel, Angelica slid closer to Raider, putting her head against his arm. The sweet perfume reached his nostrils.

Raider glared down at her. "What's on your mind, lady?"

"I want you to come with me to the hotel," she replied. "I have a surprise for you."

"Another derringer?" he asked skeptically.

She laughed coyly. "You do not understand me, cowboy. I am willing to fight for what I think is mine. Most women you know are not like me."

"And you think I belong to you?"

Her hands were in his dark hair. "For now," she whispered. "I know you will never settle down until they lower your coffin into the ground. Men like you do not grow old and play with their grandchildren."

Raider grinned. "What about women like you?"

Angelica looked around her. "Ha. To be a Mexican woman in a town like this. You don't know what it is. Where do you think Long got his start? My money. He used me. And I don't care two bits about Phoenix. I'm selling all of my interests and going back east. I only testified to get back my money."

Raider had to admire her tenacity. "How'd you get so rich, anyway?"

"Remember the cave, cowboy?"

Her inviting smile churned up a fever in Raider's body. Her breasts strained at the white fabric of her dress. She was a lot prettier than Dorie. He reined the buggy horse in front of the hotel and took her hand. She was warm to the touch.

"I'll stable this critter and go get a shave," Raider said.

"No. When the buggy is returned to the livery, come straight to my room."

"What's the number?" Raider asked, thinking he was not good at remembering. "Maybe you ought to write it down. I'd hate to get lost."

She pressed her moist lips to his, turning the heads of a few passers-by. Raider kissed her for a moment and then broke away. "Honey, we're drawin' a crowd. Save it for closed doors."

"I'm on the top floor, cowboy. Hurry. I have a whole night planned for us. You're going to repay me for saving your life."

She stepped down and strolled into the hotel. Everyone in town was envious of her, Raider thought. Women hated her because she was successful and free and beautiful. Men wanted her, plain and simple. Raider certainly found her hard to resist. He spurred the wagon toward the livery.

The shadings of late afternoon slipped into the dim corners of Phoenix. Streetlights hadn't made it yet to the town's dusty streets. A few torches burned at the end of town, where banging hammers and raspy saws worked into the evening. Raider thought some builder must be in a hurry to get a roof on a house before a rainstorm came in from the west. When he neared the stable area, Raider remembered the true purpose for all the activity. The fine citizens of Phoenix were building a gallows to hang three of their own who had done them wrong.

CHAPTER FOUR

"Lord have mercy!"

Raider's solid frame filled the threshold of Angelica's hotel room. He took off his Stetson and held it against his chest, peering into the bright, alabaster chamber. Everything was white. The walls, the curtains, the carpet, the table and chairs—even the satin dressing gown worn by his olive-skinned hostess. Angelica was sitting on a plush sofa with her crossed legs protruding from the dressing gown. Her dark hair spilled all over her shoulders, a black contrast to the virginal hue of the room's ornamentation.

Her lips parted in smile that had long forgotten innocence. "You took your time getting here, Raider."

Raider shook his head. "I reckon I would've run if I had knowed what was waitin' for me."

Angelica rose off the sofa with little effort, gliding toward Raider with the dressing gown flowing in her wake. She took the Stetson and hung it on a hook behind the door. Raider was still standing in the threshold, not exactly sure of his role in Angelica's little play-act. Her soft hands closed on his thick forearm.

"Come into my parlor, cowboy."

Her voice beckoned him into the suite. Raider stepped cautiously, as if he was afraid of soiling the white glow. Angelica offered him a seat on the sofa.

Raider hesitated. "I can't sit down there, Angel. My damned britches are covered with—"

Her finger rested on his mustache. "Don't worry, my darling one. You are my guest here. And to repay me for saving your life, you must do exactly as I say. Do you understand me?"

Raider could not take his black eyes off her face. He sat down, entranced by her brown irises. His stomach churned a little. He was wondering if she might do him dirty. After all, her testimony had condemned three men to the gallows. She seemed to be reading his thoughts.

"You are in no danger, cowboy. How could I hurt you after the things we did to each other in the cave? Let me have your boots."

Raider lifted his right leg. When Angelica stripped the boot from his foot, a hunting knife fell out onto the floor. She picked up the blade and examined it closely. Women could be damned curious about implements of destruction.

"A tool of your trade?" Angelica asked.

"Put it back in the boot."

"Yes, sir."

She dropped the knife into the boot and placed it on the floor. Raider offered his left leg. When Angelica stripped the second boot she smiled.

"No weapons?" she teased.

"I gave you that derringer that saved me," Raider replied.

"And you shall have it back—as soon as we are finished."

Raider grinned. "Take your time, lady. I ain't in no hurry."

"Nor am I. Now we must remove the gun on your hip. Would you like to stand up for me?"

Raider stood, watching Angelica as she knelt in front of him. Her hands worked the buckle of his holster, unfastening the belt that held the Peacemaker. The heavy pistol fell when the buckle was loosened.

"Easy woman," Raider said. "I just paid a gunsmith to clean and polish that hog-leg."

Angelica removed the Colt from the holster and held it in her hand. The pistol seemed gigantic in her tiny fingers. She looked up at Raider.

"What shall I do with it?"

Raider pointed toward his left boot. "Just put it down in my boot, honey."

She smiled mischievously. "Do you always keep weapons in your shoes?"

"Sometimes," he replied. "It's an old superstition. Besides, if somebody gets the drop on me, I can always pretend I'm puttin' on my boots and then . . ."

"I think I understand," Angelica said, slipping the Peacemaker into the boot. "But let's have no more talk of violence."

Raider reached for her, but she pulled away.

"No," she said. "Not yet."

"But I thought you were—"

"I want you, cowboy," she said. "But I want you my way. And remember, you are repaying a debt, so you must obey me."

"Like a damned slave?" Raider barked.

"Precisely. Just like a damned slave. Only you are condemned to pleasure, not to punishment."

Raider chortled an indecisive laugh. "All right, lady, you got it. But if things get too loco, I'm liable to cuff you one and leave you high and dry."

She opened the dressing gown, letting it fall from her shoulders. Beneath the satin garment she wore a red corset and red mesh stockings. Raider tried to catch the breath that had left him. He would have married her right then if she had asked him. He started to grab her.

"No," she teased. "My way."

"Aw, hell, where do you want me?"

She grabbed his crotch. "In the bathtub, cowboy. In the bathtub."

Raider followed her to an adjacent room where a steaming porcelain tub rested in the middle of the room. A mousy woman poured hot water from a wooden bucket. Angelica dismissed her with a nod.

"You want me to get nekkid?" Raider asked.

"I'll do that for you," she replied, reaching for the buttons of his pants. "I am going to treat you like a king, my Raider. And I intend to be your queen."

His pants, shirt, and underwear hit the floor. Raider stepped over the edge of the tub, easing himself down into the hot water. He leaned back, watching his mistress.

"The tub will take away some of the soreness," Angelica said.

"How do you know I'm sore?"

She smiled mysteriously. "I know, cowboy."

She dipped a cloth into the water and started to rub Raider's hairy chest. Her fingers were careful as she traced the mark where the cougar had scratched him. The wound was covered with a dark scab.

"Does it hurt?" she asked.

Raider shrugged. "Some. Hell, Doc put a tincture on it and burned away all of the bad stuff. He says it'll heal pretty soon."

The cloth was gliding down his stomach, toward the rigid prize that floated in the water. But Angelica did not touch him. Instead, she moved around him, rubbing his thighs. Raider grabbed her wrist and tried to guide her back to his manhood. Angelica resisted.

"You must submit to me, Raider," she said. "Otherwise I will have to ask you to leave."

Raider exhaled impatiently. He wasn't used to being bossed around by a woman. But he remembered what Angelica had done to him in the cave, when they were being chased by Harv Sturgess. So he leaned back and gave in to Angelica. It was the only way to get what he wanted.

Doc Weatherbee reclined on a feather mattress in a room that was two floors below Angelica's private chamber. He had just completed his report to the home office, detailing the affair with Harv Sturgess, as well as the trial of Long and his compatriots. The report was sealed in a large envelope that rested next to the letter that had arrived just an hour earlier. The message elaborated on the mission that awaited them in St. Louis.

Doc read the letter again, wondering how he would tell Raider about the mission. He was almost certain that Raider would not like the duty. Unlike Doc, the big man from Arkansas did not accept the home office's directives with blind loyalty. Raider always grumbled when a mission did not suit him. Of course, Raider usually complained about everything anyway, so what difference did it make if he didn't like their next assignment?

Doc rose from the mattress and looked at himself in the mirror. He was a bit more disheveled than he liked to be. Since his wallet was full of back pay, a new suit of clothes seemed to be in order. When his sartorial urges were satisfied, he would find a thick steak and perhaps a young woman.

He glanced back at the letter on the bed. Raider wasn't going to like their next assignment. So Doc decided not to tell him about it until they reached St. Louis.

"Stand up, cowboy."

Raider came out of the water, obeying Angelica's royal order. She poured a bucket of cold water over him, prompting a cry and a shudder from the big man. He wiped his eyes and glared at her.

"That cold water ain't helpin' me any," he scowled. "You done made my sidewinder lose his—"

A second bucket flowed over his thick head, Angelica laughed. "Step out of the tub, my love."

When Raider's feet hit the floor she started to dry him with a soft towel. Her touch negated the effects of the cold water. Raider looked down at the shadow of her bosom, which was pushed toward the white ceiling by the red corset. Raider lowered his mouth to hers, kissing her for a moment before she broke away.

"Damn you, woman, you're drivin' me crazy."

Her fingertips caressed his face. "I'm supposed to make you loco, Raider. And you're supposed to go along with it."

"Hell, no woman is worth this torture. You're doin' ever'-thing to me, but I ain't allowed to do a damned thing to you. If I was—"

Angelica grabbed the sack of his testicles and looked him squarely in the eye. "My way, cowboy, or you can walk out of here right now. *Comprende?*"

Raider bristled for a moment until a slight smirk materialized on his lips. She sure had him by the short hairs. But, damn it, somehow it didn't seem right for a woman to have the upper hand. Her scent wafted all around him, stunning him worse than a redwood Indian club.

"Lead me around by the nose, Angel. Go on, I'm yours."

A deep laugh from her throat. "It's not your nose that I'll use to lead you."

He followed her into the next room, where Angelica slipped a maroon silk robe over his broad shoulders. Raider didn't like the sissy feel of the thing when he first put it on, but Angelica ran her hands over his chest, feeling the smooth fabric under her fingertips, renewing his interest in her.

"So strong," she said. "So virile."

Raider wasn't sure what *virile* meant, but he didn't dwell on his ignorance. He put his hands on Angelica's shoulders, caressing her olive skin, rubbing the sides of her arms. Her body was hot to touch. He wondered how long she would be able to resist him.

"We must dine first," she said, rolling her tongue in his ear.

"You sure?"

He wanted to throw her to the floor and impale her right there.

"Our dinner is waiting," Angelica replied.

A table was sitting in the corner of the room. Angelica's servant held a sulphur match over a pair of white candles. Covered trays of silver were set in place for the meal. Angelica dismissed the servant and ushered Raider toward the table.

"Ole Doc would sure like this," Raider said.

"What?"

"Nothin'."

They sat down at the table. Raider looked over the candles at his hostess. He wanted her so much his mouth was watering. Then he realized that he smelled the fried chicken under one of the trays. His hunger overcame him, and he ate without looking at Angelica.

"Are you starving?" she asked.

"These biscuits and gravy are tolerable," he replied.

Angelica smiled. "I'm so glad you like the cuisine."

"What?"

"Here, drink some of this."

She poured a glass of dark red wine. Raider gulped it down and offered the glass for a refill. Angelica poured as fast as he would drink.

Raider drank two bottles with his dinner. Angelica had several glasses herself, but she was not drunk, or at least not as drunk as Raider. The big man was grinning from ear to ear. He pushed back from the table and belched.

"Angel, honey, if St. Peter will let you into heaven for treatin' a man right, then you ain't got nothin' to worry about."

Angelica stood up suddenly, glaring at him. "Have you so quickly forgotten our passion, cowboy?"

"Angel, what's wrong now?"

Her fingers fumbled with the strings of her corset. The red undergarment fell away, and she was standing before him naked in the candlelight. Her brown nipples were erect and firm. She turned and walked away from him, her full buttocks shifting in a vertical smirk. Raider followed her across the room, throwing off the silk robe.

He wrapped her in his arms, pressing his mouth to hers, probing with his persistent tongue. She returned the kiss, holding his broad shoulders, her breasts brushing the hair on his pectoral muscles. Raider's hands slid down her smooth back to cup her buttocks.

"Lie down on the bed," he commanded.

Her brown eyes rolled up to meet his gaze. "I am still in charge, cowboy. You lie down."

She didn't have to ask him twice. Raider sprawled back on the feather mattress, his manhood sprung to attention. Angelica joined him in bed, straddling his crotch. She took his prick in her soft hand and rolled it back and forth for a moment.

"Go ahead," Raider invited. "Have a seat."

He felt her wetness against the tip of his rigid member. He expected her to sit on him, wedging it in until the entire length disappeared inside her. But Angelica never seemed to do what he anticipated from her. She lowered her hands to the mattress and started to slide around on Raider's stomach. Her wet crotch left a sticky trail on the lines of his abdomen.

"What are you doin', girl?"

But she didn't answer, not with her mouth, anyway. Angelica slid up his chest, inching her way toward Raider's face. He caught the female scent in his nostrils. He cupped her buttocks with the intention of lifting her away from her destination.

Angelica caught his wrists. "No, cowboy. You must do what I want."

"Aw, Angel. Hell's bells. I never been one for that Frenchy stuff."

"Close your eyes. You will enjoy it."

Raider's hands fell to his sides. His head was spinning from the two bottles of wine. He took a deep breath, anticipating the musky warmth of Angelica's femininity. She took her time reaching his reluctant lips.

"Taste me, cowboy. You will not regret it."

Raider wasn't quite sure what came over him. His senses were enlivened by her. Suddenly he was seized by an unfamiliar urge to perform her bidding, not out of duty, but because he wanted to have his own oral pleasure. His tongue came out of his mouth, lapping at her crevice, charging her full body with each devilish stroke.

"Oh, cowboy, you have done this before."

But it was the first time he had actually enjoyed it! She quivered over his face, breasts and buttocks shaking, hearty gasps coming from her pretty throat. Raider was surprised when she finally pulled away. He took a deep breath and watched her put his manhood into her mouth.

Her head bobbed up and down, redoubling his pleasure as her tongue lapped at his prickhead. Raider drew his forearm across his face, wiping away her juices. She slipped off him and spread out next to him on the bed.

"I want it now," she said, pulling him. "Give me that big thing."

Raider grinned. "Now *you* want it, eh? Well, what if I ain't ready to give it to you? What if I want to torture you the same way you tortured me?"

"I know you cannot resist for long."

"Try me."

He leaned back on the pillow, his hands behind his head. Angelica fell on his chest, kissing his nipples, biting with lover's teeth. Her breasts brushed against his skin as she rolled over on top of him. She caught his cock and guided it toward her. Raider pushed her off him when he felt the result of her excitement.

"Oh no you don't," he said. "You can't get me that way."

Her eyes flared. "Just get away from me. I hate you!"

She struggled to free herself from his arms. Raider held her against the bed, working his way between her dark thighs. They wrestled until the length of his penis slid inside her. Angelica gasped and threw back her head. Raider started to move between her legs, driving in and out of her.

Their bodies bounced off the feather mattress, two entities with lives unto themselves, a man and a woman practiced in the art of love. Raider's crude energies were met by forceful thrusts from Angelica's hips. He collapsed onto her bosom, releasing his climax inside her. Angelica shuddered, cupping his buttocks to hold him within.

"Don't pull out," she begged. "Not yet."

Raider expected the hardness to return immediately, but he was wrong. Angelica looked up into his eyes. Her smile was warm and understanding.

"Isn't it better to be teased, cowboy?" she said. "Aren't you more satisfied this way? Didn't you want it more?"

"I reckon."

It was always best to agree with a woman after sex. Raider admitted to himself that he did feel contented. Angelica had been with a few men before him—her experience was proof of that. Of course, Raider had been in his share of strange beds, which made them two of a kind.

"Damn, I'm hungry again," Raider said as he rolled over.

Angelica reached for a small brass bell next to her bed. "I'll ring for the girl. Would you like more chicken?"

Raider shook his head. "Naw, but if you got some peach cobbler..."

"Done."

"With fresh cream poured over it."

The serving girl appeared to take their order. When she had disappeared, Raider gave Angelica a long kiss. She looked puzzled when he broke off.

"What was that for, cowboy?"

Raider shrugged. "Just for bein' a good woman. Boy, I tell you, I'm gonna miss this when we leave for St. Louis."

A wry smile covered Angelica's coral lips. "If you play your cards right, you can enjoy my hospitality until you arrive in St. Louis."

Raider propped himself up on his elbows. "What are you talkin' about?"

"I've arranged for you and your partner to travel with me in my private train cars," she replied. "If you'd like to share my car with me..."

"Us? Travelin' together?"

Her eyes narrowed. "Do you find that so distasteful?"

"Well, no," he stammered. "It's just that, well, Doc probably won't like it if me and you are—"

"He has already agreed. I've arranged for the transportation of his wagon and his animal. So what do you have to say to that, Mr. Raider?"

Raider threw up his hands. "Hell, I guess I can't say nothin'. You're sure as hell full of surprises. Why do you want to leave Phoenix anyway?"

She looked away from him. "I told you, I'm through with this town. I've sold all of my interests here. I'm moving east. For all I care, this town can kiss my—"

"You'd have more than one taker," Raider said. "You're about the prettiest damn woman I've ever seen."

She smiled and reclined next to him. "Thank you. We will have a glorious time together on the train. My private cars are as nice as this room."

Raider looked around at the high-class bedroom. "How'd you become such a rich lady, Angel?"

"I was married to the man who owned the sundry store," she replied. "When he died, I took over and built up the business. I was able to gather up a fair amount of holdings in Phoenix. Of course, the ladies of the town would like to spit on my grave, but I—"

"Hell, you're worth a thousand of them kind."

She kissed him. "You're not so rough as you look, cowboy."

Raider sighed. "So we're gonna be travelin' together to St. Louis, huh?"

"You sound doubtful, cowboy."

He didn't tell her that he thought traveling with women sometimes brought bad luck. He wondered if Doc had agreed to the deal just to spite him. Angelica was looking down at him with her devastating brown eyes.

"I ain't worried about a damned train ride," Raider said.

"Just think of it as partial payment for saving your life."

Looking at her healthy chest, he could not think of a better way to settle an account.

For the first time in his life, Raider was actually enjoying a train ride. Angelica's plush railroad car made it possible for him to tolerate the journey. He languished in her arms, caught up in the motion of the train, waking in the acre of a bed to make love whenever the urge struck him—or her. She was the kind of woman that might make a man quit his job and take up being a kept man.

The best part of the ride was avoiding Doc, who slept in the car behind them, when he wasn't in the livestock car singing to that infernal mule. Raider had expected his Boston-bred partner to trowel out the usual amount of grief about "professionalism" and "duty," but he was surprisingly silent. Maybe Doc knew a good thing when he saw it.

In his relaxed state, Raider noticed things about rail travel that had never reached him before. He listened, while Angelica slept, as the train rolled into deserted stations in the middle of the night. He heard the sound of the water flowing into the boiler, the chunking of coal as it fell into the coal car. Steaming whistle to mark the resumption of the journey, conductor's echoed cry in the half-light of dusk. Raider was beginning to think train travel wasn't so tedious—until the engine hissed to a stop in Emporia, Kansas.

It was just before dawn on the third day out of Phoenix. The brakes screeched, grinding the iron wheels into submission. Raider listened, expecting the sounds of water and coal. But there was only the vague murmur of muffled voices in the gray glow of morning. He sat up in bed.

Angelica rolled over and looked at him. "What is it, honey?"

"Nothin'. Go back to sleep."

She snuggled next to him, trying to initiate their loveplay. Raider pulled back the curtain and looked out the window. He saw the conductor leaning against the train. A man had a gun to the conductor's head.

"Son of a bitch."

He was reaching for his boots when the door to their chamber swung open. The man with the shotgun had a bandanna pulled over his face. Raider froze, wondering if he was a dead man.

The shotgun man had a raspy voice. "Move it, Pinkerton. And bring the Mex woman with you."

"I'm steppin' into my boots first," Raider said. "Unless you got somethin' against a man keepin' his feet warm."

Angelica raised her body. "Raider, are we—"

She saw the shotgun. When she screamed, she put her hands to her face, allowing the bedcover to fall from her breasts. Raider could not see the man's eyes, but he gambled that no man could resist a peek at Angelica's bosom. His hand went into his boot, retrieving the hidden knife. A flick of the wrist sent the blade into the man's chest. He staggered forward, dropping the scattergun. Gasping his last breaths, he tumbled to the floor.

Raider put his hand over Angelica's mouth. "Shh. Don't say nothin'. His buddies don't know he's dead yet. Just be still, you hear?"

She nodded. Raider removed his hand from her mouth. He pulled on his pants and boots and then filled his hand with the Colt .45 Peacemaker. Angelica reached for him as he started for the door.

"Sit tight, Angel. I'm gonna see if I can get us out of this."

The air was cool on his bare chest. He slipped out of the compartment and stood listening between cars. There were too many voices to count. He wedged the .45 into his pants and reached back for the scattergun. A strident voice rose above the others.

"Damon? Damon, where the hell are you? Somebody see if Damon has the woman and the Pinkerton."

Footsteps coming toward the car. Raider receded into the shadows, waiting for the dark figure to appear. When the man stepped up, Raider greeted him with the butt of the scattergun in the face. He tumbled backward, alerting the others. Raider decided to move fast. There was no other way to do it.

He flew out into the morning, hitting and rolling, coming up with the shotgun on his hip. Two flaming barrels dispatched the man who held the conductor. Gunfire flashed in the dim light, kicking up clods of dirt in front of the big man. He dropped the scattergun, running back toward the train, scuffling under the cars on his belly.

Surely Doc had heard the gunshots. Where the hell was he? A pair of legs moved to his left. Raider fired the Peacemaker into the man's crotch. When he bent over, screaming, Raider finished the job.

Voices streaked through the burnt powder. "Can't leave without the woman. . . . Run! . . . No! . . . I'm headin' out. . . ."

Hooves broke gravel behind him. Raider rolled out over the dead man, jumping to his feet. He fired at a figure moving away. The man fell from the horse. A rifle lever squeaked behind him. Another shot from a small-caliber pistol. Raider wheeled to see Doc standing over the squirming body.

"Christ Almighty, I thought you'd never get here, Doc."

Doc raised his hand to his mouth. He pointed toward the train. They stepped toward the engine, pistols in hand. Sure enough, the last man held a gun to the engineer's head.

Doc's voice was steely calm. "Pinkerton National agents. Give up before we have to terminate you."

A kid answered them in a quavering tone. "I ain't givin' up nothin'. Just let me leave with the Mex woman or this bastard gets his skull splattered."

They hesitated, wondering how to save the engineer. Before they could move another step, a metallic clanging sounded the kid's fate. The brakeman had slipped up behind him, braining him with the coal shovel. Doc and Raider climbed into the engine to look at the body.

"Caught him pretty good," Raider said. "He's gone."

Doc gestured toward the rear of the train. "Come on, we have to find the conductor and help him establish order."

The other passengers were hanging out of the windows, gawking at the carnage. The conductor was lying on the ground, holding his arm. Raider's shotgun burst had caught him in the pattern.

"I sure as hell didn't mean to wing you," Raider said. "Is he gonna be all right, Doc?"

Doc tore back the sleeve and examined the wound. "Superficial," he said. "A tincture and a bandage should have him on his feet."

The conductor smiled halfway. "Shore glad you Pinkertons was amongst us. We'd been goners for shore."

Doc glanced back at his partner. "I'm going for my medical bag. See if you can find volunteers among the passengers."

Raider scowled. "Volunteers for what?"

"To bury those bodies. After we search them, of course. I'd like to determine their identities and why they attacked this train. We weren't really carrying anything of value."

"Don't bet on it, Doc."

"Do you have a hunch, Raider?"

Raider snorted. "Let's put it this way, Doc. After the mess is cleared, I think we better talk to that whore in the fancy railroad car."

Angelica shifted nervously on the edge of the bed, clutching the lapels of a fine dressing gown. Raider paced back and forth, turning to scowl at her for a moment. He was steaming, though Doc was not sure why. He rested in a chair, waiting for his partner to take charge.

Raider pointed his finger at Angelica. "Those men knew you, lady."

She would not meet his black eyes. "No. I never saw them before in my life. They weren't after me."

Raider stomped his foot. "Bullshit. Twice they said you were Mexican. How'd they know that? And how'd they know where to find you? Huh?"

"I don't know."

Raider got close to her, right up in her face. "I want some answers, woman. You risked our lives by not tellin' us that somebody was gunnin' for you. Now I want to know who they were and why they come after this train."

Doc shifted in the chair. "Raider, perhaps we should—"

"Doc, she told me her husband was in business back there in Arizona."

The man from Boston raised an eyebrow. "Really? Did he have any partners, Mrs. Del Gado?"

She looked at the floor and nodded.

"Long," Doc continued. "The man who was hanged. Was he your late husband's partner?"

"Yes, damn you, yes!" She started to cry.

"Don't turn on the flood," Raider barked. "It ain't gonna do you no good. Just put a cork in it and tell us what we almost walked into."

Angelica dabbed at her eyes with a handkerchief. "There were three partners when my husband first went into business. I bought them out after he died. Long was one, and the other was—"

"Howard Jenkins?" Doc asked.

Angelica's brown eyes fell on him. "How did you know, Mr. Weatherbee?"

Doc reached into his coat. "I found some papers on one of the dead men. A letter from a Mr. Jenkins, listing our route of travel and a directive to bring you back to Phoenix alive."

Raider shook his head. "I'm beginnin' to see the light, Doc. She done her partners dirty, includin' sendin' one of them to hang."

"No!" Angelica cried. "It was not that way at all. After I built up the business, both men wanted back in. I . . . I was in love with Long. I let him back. He protected me from Jenkins, but he stole money as well. I was so confused, I didn't know what to do. And then . . . I don't know . . . everything was crazy. They kidnapped me and—"

"We know the rest," Raider grunted.

Doc was more gentle. "Mrs. Del Gado, why didn't you tell us that these men might make an attempt to abduct you again?"

"I was afraid you wouldn't come with me."

"You had only to request our services," Doc replied.

Raider pointed at her. "You almost got us killed."

"I'm sorry," Angelica sobbed. "Please forgive me. I would never do anything to hurt you, Raider. I . . . I love you."

"Shee-it," Raider cried. "You expect me to believe that? I'm gettin' my gear and clearin' the hell out of here."

As Raider gathered up his belongings, the train whistle blew and the steam locomotive churned out of Emporia, leaving behind blood in the sand and fresh, ummarked graves to warn would-be train robbers. Doc watched as Raider stormed out, disappearing into the next car.

Angelica was still crying. "I never meant to hurt him, Mr. Weatherbee. He will never forgive me."

Doc shrugged. "I don't blame him for being irate. If my nature were not genteel, I might harbor a grudge as well. However, since the trouble has passed without harm to myself or my partner, then I am inclined to let bygones be bygones."

"I do love him, Mr. Weatherbee. I would ask him to come east with me, but I know a man like him would never stay with one woman."

Doc agreed. "You are a perceptive, intelligent, and beautiful woman, Mrs. Del Gado. Are there any other surprises that we should know about before we arrive in St. Louis?"

"No. I'm sorry for the trouble I have caused you. I will see to it that your agency is paid handsomely. If only there were some way to get Raider back here. I . . . I am a fool."

Doc rose and patted her hand. "I wouldn't worry, my good woman. Raider's temper is volatile, but he swings back and forth. When he calms down, he may have a change of heart."

He left her sobbing into her pillow. Raider was sulking in the next car, staring out the window. Doc took the seat opposite him and struck a sulphur match to light his Old Virginia cheroot.

"Lyin' women and cigar smoke," Raider grumbled. "I hate 'em both."

Doc sat there and listened as Raider berated his former lover. The process was interesting to behold. The more he talked, the more convinced he became that he would never speak to her again. However, as evening came upon them, Raider cast wary glances toward Angelica's private car.

"Damn her. Damn that bad-luck woman!"

By nightfall, the big man was stomping back to the private car, where he would begrudgingly share the Mexican widow's warm bed.

CHAPTER FIVE

Doc Weatherbee sat patiently in the seat of his Studebaker wagon, watching as Raider said his farewells to Angelica Del Gado. Judith, Doc's mule, shifted in her harnesses, braying and scratching the dirt with her hoof. Doc brushed the flies away from her ears with a whip that was seldom used for anything else.

"You'll get your exercise, girl," he said. "As soon as Raider has finished his business."

The big man extended his palm to Angelica for an unlikely handshake. Doc smiled, thinking that the two of them had shared things much more intimate. Raider donned his Stetson as he turned away from Angelica and stepped off the platform. He was surly as he slid into the seat next to Doc.

"Get that con-sarned critter movin', Weatherbee!"

Doc shook the reins, urging Judtih through the streets of St. Louis.

Raider tipped back his hat. "What's that awful smell? You hidin' a skunk under your new derby?"

Doc laughed. "That smell is the city, my friend."

"Friend, huh?" Raider grunted. "By the way, thanks for backin' me up there in Emporia."

"You don't sound particularly grateful," Doc replied. "I did save your life, after all. Don't take it out on me because your widow—"

Raider pointed a finger in Doc's face. "Don't never say nothin' about that female again. I'm already startin' to forget her."

"My word, I believe she got to you!"

"Got to me!" Raider cried. "Hell, Doc, she only had looks, money, and tits out to here. She only wanted me to come east with her and live the good life forever. Why would that get to me?"

Doc thought that Raider's disposition would not improve when he learned the particulars of their duty. The man from Boston was silent as they rolled toward the hotel in the center of town. Raider continued to fume in his quiet way, casting hard, black-eyed glances at everything in their path.

At the hotel desk, Doc signed in, engaging two rooms near the bath. When the desk clerk, a weak-faced, balding man, looked at the signature, his nervous eyes came up to meet Doc's gaze. The clerk tugged at his starched collar as if something was wrong.

"What is it?" Doc asked.

Raider was behind him, looking over his shoulder. "We got a problem here?"

"Gentlemen," the clerk said. "Your arrival has been . . . that is . . . we weren't expecting you so soon. If I may . . . Jonathan . . ."

The man called Jonathan was broad-shouldered with red-orange hair. He came up behind the clerk, his narrow eyes cast on Doc and Raider. A bulge under his suit coat was undoubtedly a weapon. Probably a Colt pocket revolver, Raider thought. Jonathan was the trouble-shooter for the hotel.

"Are these the ones?" Jonathan asked.

"Yes. If you would be so kind as to—"

Raider leaned over the counter. "I don't know what's goin' on here, but you two frog faces are keepin' us from our work. We come here to do bi'ness with some folks, and before we do it, Doc here has to find a stable and I have to find a—"

"No need for trouble, big man," Jonathan replied in a deep voice. "You better just come along with me. I might just—"

"You might just be lookin' to step outside, red."

Doc interceded. "Raider, perhaps we should accompany this gentleman."

Raider snorted. "Doc, say the word and I'll—"

"There's no need for that," Doc replied. "If you'll tell us the nature of your request, sir, we shall be happy to follow you."

Jonathan spoke to Doc in a whisper. When he was finished, Doc turned back to Raider and nodded. Raider took his hand away from the butt of his Peacemaker. Ignoring the sign that read "No Guns Worn in Lobby," the big man fell in behind Doc and followed him to another suite on the second floor.

The suite was not elaborate, Doc thought, although some care had been taken to make the room clean. Next to the featherbed was a brocade sofa on which two diminutive figures sat waiting for them. The man called Jonathan ushered them into the chamber and then politely disappeared. Doc and Raider observed the two persons who obviously expected their arrival.

"Good day, sirs," said a small black gentleman.

He wore a dark green suit with a vest, white shirt, and tie. His curly hair was cropped short and showed signs of salt-and-pepper graying. He had a long, thin, light brown face with sorrowful eyes that came to life when he spoke. He drew on a cherrywood pipe that filled the room with a sweet tobacco smell. He stood and bowed to Doc and Raider.

"Allow me to introduce myself. I am Zebulon Freeman. Zeb, if you want to call me that."

Doc bowed in return. "I appreciate your gracious manners, sir. I am Doc Weatherbee, and this is Raider, my partner. We are the Pinkerton operatives dispatched here by our home office in Chicago. I believe we are to meet a Mr. Jacob Bolton, if I am not mistaken."

Doc glanced toward the other person on the sofa. The small figure was clad in a dark, close-fitting suit, the kind that Doc had seen on Spanish ranchers—narrow-legged trousers, short coat, frilled shirt beneath. A stiff, round leather hat with a pillbox crown covered a small head. The face and eyes were hidden beneath the wide brim.

"Are you Mr. Bolton?" Doc asked.

No reply from beneath the hat.

Raider exhaled. "I'd appreciate it if somebody would tell me what the hell's goin' on around here."

He was staring at the leather hat. A pair of green eyes flashed at him as the face turned up. Soft cheekbones and red lips. Upturned nose. Raider removed his Stetson. He was staring at a woman.

"Good afternoon, gentlemen," she said. "I am Susanna Bolton. And you will be working for me until we reach Carson City."

"Workin' for you?" Raider said.

Her smile was an unfriendly smirk. "Does it bother you to be working for a woman, Mr. Raider?"

Doc stepped in front of his partner. "I assure you, Mrs. Bolton, it does not matter to us if we work for you or your husband."

"My *father,* Mr. Weatherbee. I am Jacob Bolton's daughter. I hired you. My father didn't see the need, but I insisted."

Raider shook his head. "'Bout time somebody told me what's goin' on, Doc."

Susanna Bolton's green eyes flashed back and forth between Zeb Freeman and Raider. Her voice carried a sarcastic note. "I'd also like to know if you're adverse to working with a Negro man, Mr. Raider. Judging by the way you talk, I'd say you're one of the sons of Dixie."

Doc was looking nervous. "Miss Bolton, if you would—"

"No, Doc," Raider interrupted. "I'll speak for myself. Look here, lady." He fought the temptation to call her *girl,* because she looked old enough to be a woman. "The first thing we've got to set straight is this—don't put a 'mister' in front of my name. Call me Raider or anything else as long as you don't have 'mister' before it. Second, if you can afford to pay for havin' our services, we don't care if you're man, woman, black, or white. Hell, we'd work for an Indian if he had the money. Is that straight?"

Susanna removed her hat, allowing her red-streaked brunette tresses to fall over her shoulders. When she shifted in her suit, Raider saw the distinct impressions of pert breasts under her blouse. He grimaced as her nervous fingers produced a ready-rolled cigarette. The smoke curled over her head. She stared through Raider's black eyes.

"I don't suppose you think women should be smoking," Susanna challenged.

"Now that you mention it . . ."

Doc decided to take charge. "Miss Bolton, perhaps you should tell us why you've called us here."

Doc already knew the purpose of their mission, but he needed details. And he figured that Raider would direct his hostility at the pretty young woman if she told him the news. Doc found himself returning to stare at those green eyes.

Susanna stood up, offering the sofa to them. Zeb Freeman also got up, taking another chair across the room. Raider sat down, fighting the urge to rest his feet on the coffee table in front of the sofa.

Susanna paced back and forth as she spoke. "I suppose I must seem strange to you gentlemen. I've been living back east, you see, and things are much different there. After all, it is 1879—"

"We know the date," Raider said. "Just get to the meat."

Susanna cast a disapproving glance at the big man. "Perhaps you've heard of my father, Jacob Bolton. He has mining interests in Nevada and California. Near the border."

"I ain't heard of him, Doc. Have you?"

"Silence, Raider. Let Miss Bolton continue."

"Thank you, sir," she replied. "You see, unlike some men who inhabit the western states and territories, my father is a gentleman. He comes from a long line of gentlemen, in fact. Our family history can be traced back to the *Mayflower* landing."

"Mayflower?" Raider said.

"I'll explain later," Doc replied. "Continue, Miss Bolton."

She smiled at Doc. "I'm sure *you* understand what I'm talking about, Mr. Weatherbee."

"Call me Doc."

"Yes, of course. Where was I?"

Raider lifted his feet onto the coffee table. "You was tellin' us that your pappy is some kind of gentleman who likes flowers and such."

Her green eyes decided to ignore Raider. She looked directly at Doc as she continued. "It is my father's proper breeding that has prompted his recent attempts to bring the accoutrements of the East to the West. You see, in Carson City, where he has been living for the last ten years, there are very few of the finer things in life. My father has built himself a wonderful house in a green valley just outside Carson City. He lives the life of a gentleman, but I'm afraid he's a bit bored."

Doc smiled. "Are you bored as well?"

"Heavens no," she replied. "I've been going to school in Lexington, Kentucky. Father sent me east five years ago, when I was nineteen. He didn't think it was right for a young lady to stagnate in Carson City. Of course, I didn't want to go at first, but I'm glad that I did. That's why the trip back is doubly important for me. It's a homecoming of sorts. I haven't seen my father in five whole years."

Raider grunted. "He'll be glad to see that you're smokin' and wearin' men's clothes."

"Keep your opinions to yourself, Mr. Rai . . . Raider."

"Sure enough," the big man replied. "So your daddy wants us to baby-sit you on the trip west, huh? Think we can handle that, Doc?"

Doc nodded toward Susanna. "There's more, Raider."

"Much more," Susanna continued. "You see, to help relieve the boredom of the Nevada wilderness, my father has seen fit to sponsor a stakes race."

"A what?" Raider asked.

"A horse race," Susanna replied. "An 'all-comers' stakes race. A challenge to any horse west of the Mississippi. The race will be run three weeks from yesterday, as part of a celebration to commemorate the twenty-year anniversary of the Comstock Lode. People from all over the territory will be there."

"Sounds cozy," Raider interjected. "But where do we fit in to this shindig?"

Susanna stubbed out her ready-rolled and crossed her arms. "If you would allow me to finish."

"Hell, yeah, go right on."

Doc dug an elbow in Raider's ribs. "Excuse him, Miss Bolton. He hasn't any manners, but you will find him capable in a pinch."

"Thank you, Doc. Please call me Susanna."

"Yes, Susanna. If you will continue."

She took a deep breath and locked her hands together. "Oh, my father. He's a rather imaginative sort. A dreamer. You see, when his mining interests paid off, he found himself with very little to do but count his money. He tried hunting and fishing, and practically everything else. But alas, he sees himself as a squire, riding to the hounds. He's very excited about this race. In his last letter he told me that the purse for the race is up to ten thousand dollars—winner take all."

Raider sat up, removing his boots from the table. "Is your daddy puttin' up that money hisself?"

"All of it," Susanna said proudly.

Raider looked at Doc. "He must have a hell of a filly to run for him."

"A stallion," Susanna corrected. "One of the best, right Zeb?"

The black man smiled and nodded. "Eastern Star is a fine horse. I should know. I raised him from a colt."

"Zeb is Star's trainer and jockey," Susanna replied. "He's going to ride Star in the stakes race for my father. It should be exciting to see those western-breds challenging a Kentucky thoroughbred. Worth every penny, too. My father paid two thousand for Star."

Raider cringed. "Two thousand bucks for a horse?"

"Not just any horse," Susanna replied. "Star has a bloodline that goes all the way back to Diomed."

"Dio-what?"

"Diomed," Doc rejoined. "Winner of the Epsom Derby, a stallion without parallel. Brought to America from England in the early part of this century to sire many foals at the ripe old age of twenty-one."

Zeb Freeman smiled at Doc. "You know your horseflesh, Mr. Weatherbee. What would you say to me if I mentioned the name Aristides?"

"Winner of the first Kentucky Derby. Sired by Leamington out of Sarong. Ran the mile and a half at the Derby in under two minutes forty seconds."

"Two minutes, thirty-seven and three-quarter seconds," Susanna said. "Star is one of the colts sired by Aristides."

"Then I'd say he's probably swift of hoof," Doc replied.

Raider's black eyes had narrowed. He looked at Doc and then at the woman. It was starting to sink into his thick head.

"Where is this horse?" he asked.

"Right here in St. Louis," Susanna replied.

Raider stood up. "You mean we come all the away from Arizona to play nursemaid to some overpriced hayburner?"

Doc looked up at his partner. "Please, Raider, wait until you've heard all the facts. Susanna, why did your father summon us? I must say that I share my partner's concern in this matter. If we are merely going to act as bodyguards to Eastern Star, there are men who will do it for less money—quite capable men, I might add."

Susanna looked away from them. "My father was against hiring the Pinkerton Agency. But I insisted. You see, when we brought Star from Kentucky, Zeb caught two men trying to get into the livestock car where Star was resting. I don't know what they were after, but I thought it best to hire someone to oversee the trip west. We cannot afford to lose Star, not with the importance of this race. My father would lose too much money if something happened to his horse."

Doc's brow was wrinkled. "Why did your father protest the hiring of the Pinkerton Agency to guard his investment?"

Susanna sighed. "He thinks I'm being overly concerned."

Raider looked at Freeman. "Did you recognize them boys that was tryin' to break into the livestock car?"

"No, I can't say that I did," Freeman replied.

"You think they was up to no good?"

"I can't be sure. But I do believe that Susanna is right. We should have some protection on the trip west."

"What about the former owners?" Doc asked. "Do you think they might try to steal back their horse?"

Freeman sat up straight. "I can vouch for the McKnight family. They are one of the proudest families in all of Kentucky. They would never welch on a deal or try to cheat anyone. The only reason they sold Star to begin with was a shortage of funds to run their breeding farm. Mr. Bolton offered them a price that they could not turn down. It hurt them greatly, too, since Star will never run in the Derby now."

"Still," Doc said, "we can't rule out any suspect if there is foul play. Miss Bolton, would you mind if I spoke to my partner alone for a moment?"

"Not at all. Zeb and I are planning to run Star this afternoon. If you would like to come along, feel free to accompany us. We'll be leaving within the hour."

She cast a wary glance at Raider and then strode out of the room with Freeman behind her. Raider shook his head. They were sure an unlikely pair. Doc seemed puzzled as well.

"What do you think, Raider?"

The big man scratched his head. "Hell, Doc, I don't rightly know. You want to play nurse to a damned pony?"

"It does sound that way," Doc replied, rubbing his chin. "However, we can't overlook two things: first, the attempt to break into the rail car where the horse was riding; second, the worth of the animal."

"A hundred double eagles for a horse," Raider sighed. "Shit, I've had to shoot my mount and eat it. That'd be an expensive meal. I wonder why her daddy didn't want us along for the ride?"

Doc nodded. "That does seem strange. Although, I daresay a man does not take his daughter as seriously as a son. He probably thinks her woman's intuition is too active."

"What do you think about her, Doc?"

"Pretty. Impetuous. Not as mature as she wants to believe. Good at the core. A bit spoiled. Lovely, though."

Raider laughed. "Hell, Doc, it sounds like you're sweet on her."

Doc's face turned a bright shade of red. "You asked for my opinion; I simply gave it to you."

"Easy, Doc. Easy. I didn't mean nothin'."

Doc stood up. "We have two alternatives, as I see them. One, we can wire the home office and have them take us off the case. Two, we can proceed as directed. Anyone could probably handle this thing without too much trouble. Of course . . . no, I don't think that would apply here."

Raider looked sideways at his partner. "You got that look on your face, Doc. You're thinkin' somethin', and I want to know what it is."

"Forget it, Raider."

"Tell me, Doc, or me and you are goin' round and round."

Doc took in a breath. "Well, have you ever watched the current of a river and seen a small piece of wood sticking up out of the water?"

"Yeah. Who hasn't?"

"And when you waded out to that small piece of wood, did you sometimes find that it was attached to a whole tree that was hiding beneath it?"

Raider groaned. "No riddles, Doc. Just spill it."

"How many times have we accepted a simple case, only to find that there was more to it than meets the eye?"

Raider slapped his leg. "Hell, Doc, you're just tryin' to talk me into somethin' that I don't want to do."

"Very well, then you can send the wire to Allan Pinkerton, telling him that you would like to request assignment for both of us to another case."

"Shit fire." Raider scowled. "I don't know what to do."

Doc grinned devilishly. "The decision is yours."

"Aw, doggone it."

"I'm waiting for an answer, Raider."

"You win, Doc. Let's go look at a two-thousand-dollar horse."

"Isn't he beautiful?" asked Susanna Bolton.

Doc and Raider leaned over the railing of an abandoned horse track, taking in the majestic chestnut figure of Eastern Star. They had ridden in the Studebaker to a stable five miles west of St. Louis. Two men with rifles stood beside them, making sure no harm came to the muscular stallion. Both of the Pinkerton operatives were stunned by the presence of the Kentucky-bred horse. No three-year-old colt west of the Mississippi could touch him for form, Raider thought.

"Some hunk of horse, Miss Bolton," Raider said, tipping back his Stetson. "Or do you want me to call you Susanna?"

"No, Miss Bolton will do nicely."

Raider laughed and turned to his partner. "What do you say about that pony, Yankee man? Or did you learn about horses in Boston?"

Doc didn't even hesitate. "A fine specimen of Kentucky breeding. Short, sturdy cannon bones, hooves parallel, pointing straight ahead. Long neck, good angle from fetlock to hoof, hind pasterns perfect. Shoulders are long as well, deep chest. I can never remember seeing an animal this fine."

Susanna slipped her arm into Doc's. "Remarkable. How about his weight?"

"Nine hundred seventy?"

She smiled, pleasantly surprised at Doc's knowledge. "Nine seventy-five."

"Fifteen hands three, I'd say," Raider chimed in.

He could see she was going for Doc, but he wasn't going to look the fool. He knew a little bit about horses. There was more to running a race than showboating. A racer had to have fire in his eyes.

"Can he run, little lady?" Raider challenged the upturned nose.

"I'll let you see for yourself. Zeb? All right."

Freeman hung in the tiny saddle aboard Eastern Star. Raider realized just how small the man was when he saw him on the horse's back. The black man urged Star into a walk. Slabs of firm muscle shifted under the colt's reddish-gold hide.

"Did he get his name from that mark on his forehead?" Doc asked.

Susanna looked puzzled. "I don't know."

"That's a star all right," Raider said. "Although it looks more like a diamond to me. Funny, that's the only white mark on him. I saw a horse like that once. He was—"

Freeman moved on Star's back. The horse shot forward, bolting for the first turn of the mile track. Raider tilted over the rail, following the streak of red-gold that flew into the back stretch of the track. Doc held his pocket watch in hand, timing the stallion's flight.

"That damned Freeman knows how to ride," Raider cried. "Whoo-wee."

Eastern Star rounded the final turn, driving for an imaginary finish line. Doc kept looking at his watch and then glancing up at the streaming mane. His watch was not exact, but he was quite sure that Eastern Star had run a mile in well under two minutes. Raider raised his hands to applaud.

Susanna looked at Doc's watch. "What?"

"A minute fifty-five," Doc replied. "But I'm only guessing."

"I don't know about times, but that's the best-lookin' race-horse I ever saw." Raider clapped Doc on the back. "I told you this was gonna be a good mission, Doc."

The big man was suddenly all smiles.

Doc caught on pretty quick. "You like Eastern Star, don't you, Raider?"

Susanna smiled triumphantly. "You surely had a change of

heart. Is he being rude, Doc? Or is he sincere?"

"He wants to *bet* on Eastern Star," Doc said.

Raider feigned innocence. "Me? Bet on a horse? You oughta know better than that, Doc. I never risk my money."

"Why wouldn't you bet on Star?" Susanna asked, showing him her aristocratic, arrogant pout.

"Lady," Raider said, "ain't no horse west of here gonna beat that stallion in any kind of race, anywhere, any day. Nope, bettin' on that boy ain't gonna be no risk at all. It's a sure thing. Your daddy done seen to that."

Susanna slapped him, though not very hard. "I find you insolent, crude, and uncouth. You could stand to have a few more manners, like your partner here."

Raider jabbed Doc's arm with a friendly tap. "If I had a dollar for ever' time I heard that . . ."

Freeman came up next to them with Eastern Star. The colt was barely puffing. He had a light lather from the workout. Susanna reached up to touch the diamond-shaped star on the animal's forehead. Star snorted and moved back a little.

"I'm taking him back into the stable," Freeman said. "I'll rub him down. I'm going to stay here with him tonight. I don't like the way this stable is built. He might get too cold at night."

Susanna shook her head. "I'm sorry about the accommodations, Zeb. The money didn't arrive at the Western Union today." She turned to Doc. "They use this place in the spring, for the races at the county fair. It's the best I could do."

"And your father was supposed to send you money?" asked Doc.

"Yes, and I'm sure it will get here. He's just so busy, getting the celebration organized."

Doc nodded. Susanna squeezed his bicep and started toward the stable. Raider leaned back against the railing. The two rifle men were looking at him. Raider gave them a wave of his hand.

"We're takin' over now, partners."

They were staring at Raider. "She owes us money."

Raider shrugged. "You'll get it."

"We're wantin' to move on. Now."

Doc reached into his pocket, withdrawing his wallet. "How much do you have coming to you?"

"Five dollars. Each one of us."

Doc gave them script. They were both satisfied. As they left, Raider turned to his partner. Raider could not believe that Doc, a tightwad usually, had parted with his hard-earned money.

"You must be sweet on her to pay them off like that, Doc.".

Doc put his hand on Raider's shoulder. "Partner, how long has it been since we had a fistfight?"

Raider's smirk vanished. "You tryin' to make a point?"

"I like Miss Bolton—immensely. I've never asked you for anything, Raider. I'm asking you now to leave Susanna alone. She's a young, vulnerable girl."

Raider chortled. "That bitch! Shit, she loves bein' hateful. I—"

"Raider, if you keep up, you're going to make me mad, and then I'm going to hit you, and then we're both going to be sorry that we got into it."

Raider shook his head. Doc made sense, though. It was better to avoid a scuffle. Even if it did mean that Raider had to act respectful.

"Okay, Doc. But if she comes after me . . ."

Doc persisted. "No. Treat her like you would a queen. Just indulge her. I get the feeling that she's under a great deal of pressure."

Raider didn't like the tone of Doc's voice. "Why you talkin' all low and spooky-like, Doc? This thing is a cinch. Run the pony out to Nevada, bet like a sin, and cash in our tickets."

"Remember the tree in the river."

Susanna called to Doc, inviting him into the stable area. Raider came behind him. They slid through a narrow doorway into the dimly lit stable. As Raider ducked under the threshold, he heard a low wailing, followed by the clicking of claws above him. A black cat sailed down off the stable loft, landing on his shoulder. Raider knocked the cat away and drew his Colt.

"No!" Susanna cried. "Don't shoot!"

Raider took aim on the cat. Susanna grabbed his wrist. He looked down into her frantic green eyes.

"That damned thing scratched me," Raider said. "You don't want it around here, scaring that horse. It might have rabies."

Susanna glanced back at the cat. "Just watch."

"Dad-blamed bad-luck cat!"

The shifty feline skulked back toward the stall where Freeman had begun to groom Eastern Star. Leaping up onto the low wall, the cat perched in front of the chestnut stallion, swishing its bushy tail back and forth. Star swung his head and nuzzled the fuzzy creature.

"Shadow Cat," Susanna said. "He's Star's best friend. Makes him run faster."

Raider could not believe it. "You mean that prize racehorse loves a mangy critter that I almost blasted?"

Doc stepped between Raider and Susanna. "Thoroughbreds have been known to have companions," he said. "They become attached to a smaller animal."

Raider holstered his .45. "That sounds like some bullshi . . . somethin' that ain't even true."

Susanna gloated. "Believe your eyes, cowboy."

"Yes, ma'am," Raider replied politely.

He was going to respect Doc, even if it killed him.

They moved to the stall, getting a closer view of the stallion. Doc reached out to pet the cat, but Shadow Cat knocked his hand away. Bared teeth and a hiss from Star's best friend.

"He don't like you neither, Doc."

Freeman dragged a brush over the chestnut's neck. "That kitty goes ever'where we go. I don't know why, but Star loves him better than anything. Had a chicken before the cat come, but Star never liked that chicken too much."

Raider leaned over the stall. "What happened to the chicken?"

Freeman laughed. "Cat killed him."

They all laughed until Susanna Bolton slid next to Doc and asked, "Who's going to stay with Star tonight?"

Raider frowned. "I thought Freeman was stayin'."

"No," Doc rejoined, "Susanna is right. One of us should remain here. And since you fired the other hands, Raider, I think you should be the one to do it."

"I get to skin the week-old buffalo, huh?"

Raider wondered if he wanted to risk a fistfight for a night in the hotel. He looked around the stable. He had stayed in dirtier, smellier places. And there was something funny in Doc's expression, in the way he looked at the girl. Not like he wanted her, but like he was afraid for her. Doc seemed to know about eastern women.

"All right, Doc, I'll guard the pony."

Even with that bad-luck cat, he was going to stay.

"Isn't the moon lovely?"

Susanna Bolton, clad in a white dress, was staring up at the sky. The riding clothes had not done her justice. Doc, who was decked out in a freshly pressed suit, slid his arm around her. They had stopped on the wooden sidewalk between the restaurant and the hotel to admire the firmament. Doc had enjoyed a fine dinner, complete with a rare bottle of French wine. The scent of Susanna's hair made him light-headed.

"You should see the moon on the prairie," Doc said.

"I have," she replied. "Remember, I lived in Nevada most of my life."

"I'd forgotten. Though it is hard to imagine a petite lady like you on the plain."

She pulled him forward, walking again. "Mr. Weatherbee, I want to thank you for paying for my supper. As soon as my money arrives..."

"Think nothing of it."

She slid her arm around his waist. "Think of it as expenses that you will be reimbursed."

He stopped her and spun her around to face him. She smiled. Doc took her chin in hand and bent to kiss her. She returned the sentiment, but only for a moment. She ran her hand over Doc's sandy hair.

"You're a kind man, Mr. Weatherbee."

"I cannot tell you how much I have enjoyed your company, Miss Bolton."

They resumed their stroll, arm in arm.

"I don't know why Father hasn't sent my money," Susanna said. "He was always on time when I was at school."

Doc sensed a hesitancy in her voice when she spoke about money. He wondered if he should tread into sensitive ground. He decided to plunge forward.

"Miss Bolton, your father has probably incurred some large expenditures with the raising of the stakes money and so forth. Perhaps your money has been delayed because he's having financial troubles."

Her arm disappeared from his waist. "I doubt that, Mr. Weatherbee."

"Well," Doc offered, "you have been away for several years. I don't mean to pry, but it would help me to know the state of . . ."

Susanna stepped away from him. "It would help you to know only what I tell you, Mr. Weatherbee. You are a hired man, not a confidant."

"Do you always kiss the hired men?"

She slapped him hard. "I knew you would try to boss me if I let you kiss me. Men never respect me. They all tell me what to do."

"I was only thinking of your own safety, Susanna. Eastern Star is a very valuable horse, to you and your father."

Tears were streaking down her cheeks. "Good night to you, Mr. Weatherbee."

"Miss Bolton, I was only trying to . . ."

But it was too late, she was already halfway to the hotel, storming along under the gaslights. Doc sighed. Susanna was not as confident as she appeared. Perhaps she knew something that she was not telling Doc. Or sensing something that she could not tell him. He would wait her out. Even though it might be a very icy trip to Carson City.

"That sure was some good whiskey, Freeman."

Raider leaned against the wall of the stable, passing a flask back to the diminutive black man. They both had a good view of Eastern Star's stable. Two lamps were burning to light the enclosure. Freeman pulled down the last of the red-eye. They were both a little tight.

"Tell me somethin', Freeman," Raider said. "Is that really the fastest racehorse you ever saw?"

Freeman nodded, his face lined in the flickering of the flame. "Yes, sir, old Star is the finest. I seen 'em too, seen Aristides himself. I was s'posed to ride in the Derby that day, but I hurt my leg in the race before the big one."

"Can I make some money on this horse?"

Freeman laughed. "Well, the race ain't always to the fastest, but that's the way to bet."

"Damned if it ain't."

A boot crushed straw outside the stable. Raider stood up and drew his Colt. Freeman's eyes were wide. Raider thumbed back the hammer of the .45.

"Who the hell is out there?"

Doc Weatherbee's voice came through a knothole. Raider holstered the pistol and slid down the wall. His partner slipped in through the narrow door. He tipped his derby to both of them.

Raider grinned. "Didn't go too well with the lady, huh?"

Doc did not smile. "I hope you didn't shoot the cat yet. And by the way, you aren't supposed to drink on duty."

"Write me up and send me in," Raider replied.

Doc ignored him. "I made arrangements for the train. We'll have a private car behind the livestock car where Star will be riding. My wagon and mule will be in the front half of Star's quarters."

Raider snorted. "Seems kinda like a sin to give this horse such a fancy send-off."

Freeman was looking at Doc. "Did Miss Susanna's money come yet, Mr. Weatherbee?"

Doc shook his head. "No. I made the arrangements through our office. Mr. Freeman, do you know anything about Jacob Bolton's finances?"

"I don't want to say nothin', sir."

Raider looked at Freeman. "Say it. We don't like nothin' to come out of the blue. We like to know about somethin' before it happens."

"I don't know," Freeman said. "I seen the girl's daddy when he bought this horse. He was a worried man. Didn't even much care about Star. Paid me extra to come along. I'm goin' back to Kentucky when the race is over."

"Did you get all of your money?" Doc asked.

Freeman shook his head. "Give me half. Said he'd give me the other when I come to Nevada."

"Why didn't you ask him for all of it?" Raider inquired.

"Black man don't ask a white man for money," Freeman replied. "Not unless he wants trouble."

Raider frowned at his partner. "You gettin' at somethin', Doc?"

"No, just prying. Can you tell me anything else about Jacob Bolton or how you got hooked up with his daughter?"

Freeman shook his head emphatically. "I ain't hooked up with no one but the McKnight family. I'm their head groom and stable man. I just came along because it's one last chance to ride a great horse. I don't know the business of the Bolton's, and besides riding Eastern Star, I don't want to know."

"Leave him alone, Doc."

They were quiet for a moment. The cat sauntered over the straw and curled up at the feet of Eastern Star. Raider grinned, thinking of all the money he would win.

"I'm tellin' both of you, no western-bred is gonna outrun this chestnut. You hear me, Freeman? Doc?"

Freeman laughed. "I'll guess we'll see when we get to Nevada."

Raider looked at his partner, but Doc was not smiling. The man from Boston was frowning at the black cat that lay curled in a pile of straw across the stable.

CHAPTER SIX

Doc Weatherbee stood between two railroad cars, smoking an Old Virginia cheroot, thinking how smoothly the trip had gone so far. They had left St. Louis in the early morning, making Kansas City just at nightfall. The pair of private cars, one for Eastern Star and Judith, the other for human passengers, were transferred to a northern-bound train in Kansas City. Doc wanted to pick up the St. Paul-Pacific in Omaha, for a route through the central states and territories.

They hit Denver on the night of the third day, but broke down between Cheyenne and Laramie, just over the Wyoming border. A tense half day had passed while the boiler was adjusted. Eastern Star's friend, the black cat, had added to their distress by leaving the train to pounce on a ground squirrel. Luckily the pampered feline returned to Star's boxcar before the train chugged on through the foothills of Medicine Bow and the Rockies.

Purple slopes rose on both sides of the train as the St. Paul line twisted a serpentine path through a shaded pass. Doc leaned against the door of his private car and took a deep breath. He felt safer in the mountains, even though Raider said it was the most likely place for an ambush. His partner had spent most of his time in the livestock car with Freeman and Eastern Star. Raider said he preferred a horse's company to Susanna Bolton's.

Miss Bolton had been extremely quiet and distant during the journey. Doc ignored her behavior, treating her with civility when he had to speak to her. He was waiting her out, hoping she would be honest with him about her father's finances, even though it might not mean much to their task at hand.

"Ain't this train smoky enough for you, Doc?"

Doc raised his eyes toward the roof of the boxcar. Raider stood in the shadows rendered by the high peaks of the mountains. The big man climbed down a narrow steel ladder. Doc stubbed out the stogie and stored the butt in a silver case that went back into his vest pocket. He straightened his derby and regarded his partner.

"I trust everything is secure in the livestock car."

Raider shrugged. "Horse hockey and harmonica playin'. That damned Freeman knows ever' song that was wrote. You see anything up this way?"

Doc shook his head. Raider leaned out to peer ahead of the train. They were winding into a gap that left little room on either side of the track. Raider shivered.

"Don't like the mountains one bit, Doc."

"I wouldn't worry," Doc replied. "Our caravan was most vulnerable in Kansas City, when we were changing to the new engine. We'll hit Salt Lake City in the morning and should be on our toes. From there we'll be in the great basin. We have no reason to worry."

Raider pulled out his .45 and spun the chamber on his sleeve. "We still gonna git off in Reno?"

Doc nodded. "We have to. The train ends there. It won't be a long ride to Carson City."

"I know," Raider said. "I been in this part of the country before. What are we gonna do with the stallion?"

Doc shrugged. "He'll have to walk like the rest of the animals."

"I'll tell Freeman and see what he says." He started to go up the ladder. Doc stopped him.

"Stay here for a while, Raider, if you will. I'm going into

the car for a cup of coffee."

Raider grinned. "Just can't stay away from her, can you, Doc?"

Doc shot him a dirty look. Raider turned back toward the rocky slopes. "By the way, Doc, where the hell are we?"

"Between Green River and Rock Springs," Doc called as he closed the door behind him.

Raider holstered his .45 and leaned back against the door. He couldn't understand what Doc saw in the brunette. She was awful skinny. And as far as Raider could tell, Susanna Bolton liked being a bitch.

When Doc entered his private compartment, Susanna Bolton was waiting for him. She had abandoned her coat and trousers—what Raider called a Mexican monkey suit—for a high-necked cotton dress that made her look more like a schoolgirl. She blushed when she met Doc's eyes. She turned away, pretending to look out the window. Doc sat down in the opposite seat and waited for her to break the ice.

"Mr. Weatherbee."

Still not looking at him.

"Yes, Miss Bolton."

"Mr. Weatherbee." She extended her smooth, pale hand. "I want you to have this. It was my mother's."

Doc took a ring from her palm. He lifted it into the afternoon light to see that it was a fine emerald stone in a gold setting. His eyes fell on Susanna's pretty face.

"I don't understand, Miss Bolton. Why are you giving this to me?"

She stared down at the floor. "For expenses. Please, don't make this difficult for me. I am ashamed enough as it is."

"Look at me, young lady."

She responded instantly to the authoritative tone in Doc's voice. Her green eyes were opened wide. Doc gave her back the ring.

"I will settle with your father," he said. "Since you have chosen not to be completely honest with me, I will take this matter up with Jacob Bolton himself."

She reached forward and took his hands. "Don't be angry with me, Doc. I'm worried. My father said my money would be there before I left St. Louis."

"And it never arrived. I know. Why do you think I made the travel arrangements myself? Of course, your father must reimburse the agency for every expense."

"And I'm sure he will."

Doc was deliberately skeptical. "Are you certain?"

Susanna began to cry. Doc moved next to her, slipping his arm around her shoulder. She rested her head on his chest, sobbing.

"I'm so afraid, Doc. I haven't heard from my father since we left Lexington. He put me in charge of getting Eastern Star to Carson City, but I ran out of money in St. Louis. I was going to sell this ring, but I couldn't. It was given to me by my mother, right before she died. I was only a little girl."

In many ways she was still a little girl, Doc thought. He touched her cheek, fighting his urge to kiss her. He could not take advantage of her in such a weakened state.

"Miss Bolton, it is my job to try to set things right, if indeed things have gone wrong. Your father's oversight in not sending your money could be directly related to his sponsoring a stakes race. There are quite a number of details that he might find . . . distracting."

She looked up at him, tears furrowing in her cheeks. "I thought the same thing."

Doc smiled. "Is there anything else that I should know about this race?"

"You know as much as I do."

Doc gave her his handkerchief. He found it odd that her father would leave her stranded with no funds. She did seem like a resourceful young woman, but Eastern Star was a great responsibility. Perhaps there had been a foul-up with the wire service, or maybe Susanna had simply mismanaged her budget for the trip west.

"I suppose I'm worrying needlessly," Doc said. "Looking for things that aren't there."

"Mr. Weatherbee?"

"Yes, Susanna?"

"Will you kiss me again?"

Her eyes were closed. Her lips were pursed in a girlish pucker. Doc could not help himself. When he lowered his mouth to hers, she came alive, running her hands over Doc's shoulders as they embraced. Doc felt her breasts against his chest, the firm nipples tight inside her cotton dress.

Doc broke away. "Quite enough, Susanna."

She looked hurt. "Don't you like me?"

"Yes. But..."

She tried to kiss him again. Doc grabbed her wrists and held her away from him. If things went any further, he might lose control.

"Susanna, you are under distress right now. You aren't sure of your... your feelings toward me."

"I think you're handsome, Doc. And a real gentleman."

Doc blushed. "Thank you. However, a real gentleman does not take advantage of a confused, twenty-one-year-old girl."

She stood up. "I'm a twenty-two-year-old woman."

"Please." Doc rose and held her arms. "Susanna, let's make a pact. When we arrive in Carson City, you will have time to sort out this matter. Until then, we can remain friends. I do like you immensely."

"Then why won't you kiss me?"

"Because a kiss may lead to more—"

Her green eyes flashed at him. "I'm not a virgin, if that's what you're thinking, Doc. I—"

"Enough! Honestly, Miss Bolton, this kind of talk is quite improper for a young lady."

Doc grabbed his derby and fled from the compartment. He hurried outside, where Raider was still standing between the cars. The big man was smiling like a possum on an abandoned honey tree.

"Got rouge on your shirt, Doc."

Doc scowled at his partner. "Don't say another word."

"Just thought you might like to know about the rouge."

Raider reached for the ladder. Doc fished for the remains of the stogie. He struck a match as Raider started to climb.

"I'll be in the horsecar, Doc," he called back.

Doc grunted and blew out a puff of smoke. "We'll be in Green River soon. See that you're alert."

Raider stepped onto the top of the boxcar and started walking on the roof of the train. The livestock car was fixed on the back of the train, behind the caboose. Doc had tried to get the railroad to put the horse car in the middle, but regulations required a passenger train to keep all livestock behind the other cars. It was just Raider's luck to be the only one who had to endure the stink.

He jumped over from the private car to the caboose. The cars rocked a little as he climbed down the ladder to the livestock car. Freeman was sitting by the door with an old Kentucky squirrel rifle, a .29 caliber. Raider sat down next to him in the straw.

"You sure you know how to shoot that thing, Freeman?"

The black man laughed. "If I can hit a squirrel, I surely ought to be able to knock the eye out of a man's head."

"Don't talk like that," Raider replied. "We got enough bad luck with that cat runnin' around, so don't talk up nothin'."

Freeman shook his head. "You think that cat is bad luck 'cause of his color. Well, Mr. Raider, I happen to think he's got a good color on him. He always brung me luck."

"I hope you're right."

"You wait," Freeman said, shaking his finger. "You'll see how my luck runs. I'm a lucky man."

Raider picked up his Winchester and clicked a round into the chamber. "Mr. Freeman, sometimes a man has to make his own luck."

"You talk enough for both of us."

Freeman raised his harmonica to his lips and started to blow a mournful tune.

Raider grimaced. "Don't you know somethin' lively?"

But Freeman kept right on playing. Eastern Star snorted in his stall. The black cat was on his back, curling up for a nap. Maybe that damned horse liked the music, Raider thought. He just hoped the dreary melody would make Star run faster. Especially when it came time to make a wager.

Doc was still riding between the cars when the brakes screeched in Green River, Wyoming. He stepped off the motionless train, glancing back at the livestock car. Raider emerged from the side and stretched his arms. Then he slipped through a crack in the door, wriggling his way to the roof of the car. When his Winchester was on his hip, he waved to Doc.

Doc yelled back, "Check all directions."

Raider jumped onto the caboose and hurried toward the engine, leaping from car to car until he was looking down into a ton of coal. As he came back toward the livestock car, he gave Doc the high sign. Doc motioned toward the rear of the train. Raider leapt over to the caboose, leaving his partner to cover the car that carried Susanna. As he neared the livestock car, he heard Freeman's agitated voice.

"I caught him, Mr. Raider. He was snoopin' around."

Freeman held his squirrel rifle on a man with a lantern. The man wore an engineer's cap and the company bandanna for the St. Paul line. His hands were raised over his head.

"Tell this boy not to shoot me," the man said.

Raider climbed down the iron ladder to the ground. He held up the Winchester in the man's face. He looked like a railman.

Raider nodded to Freeman. "Where'd you find him?"

"Snoopin' between cars. I heard him first."

The railman dropped the hand that held the lantern. "I'm just checkin' the cars, sir. I'm supposed to on every train that passes by here. There's a right nasty mountain up there. We lost more than one car that broke loose on that slope."

Freeman was not ready to trust him. "Call your partner, Mr. Raider. He should talk to this man."

"Doc!"

The man from Boston hurried back along the tracks. He took in the situation with his hand on his chin. Raider gestured with the muzzle of the Winchester.

"Doc, this boy says he's a trainman, checking the cars 'cause they got a bad hill up yonder."

Doc peered up toward the fading purple slopes. "It makes sense," he said. "I'll get the conductor to check his work. Hold him here while I—"

The train whistle sounded. A conductor came out of the caboose, holding up a lantern in the twilight. Raider grabbed the railman's arm and pushed him forward into the light of the conductor's lantern.

"You know this man?" Raider asked.

The conductor held out the lantern over the railman's hat. "Can't say that I've seen him before. Could be the new man."

Doc gestured toward the connection between the cars. "He says he was checking this rigging because of a rather arduous incline in the mountains."

The conductor nodded. "Yeah, he's just doin' his job."

"You the new man?" Raider asked.

He was right up in the railman's sweaty face.

"I'm the new man, yessiree. That gun scares me, sir."

The conductor laughed. "They ain't gonna hurt you, son. They're Pinkerton agents. What's your name, boy?"

"Thompson," the railman replied. "Eli Thompson."

"Welcome aboard, Eli," the conductor said. He swung the lantern along the side of the train. "And all aboard for you, gentlemen."

Doc and Raider stepped up onto the train. The engine lurched forward, steaming and hissing in the cool night air. Freeman ran alongside the car until Raider reached down and pulled him up. He couldn't have weighed more than a hundred pounds. For Eastern Star, it would be like carrying a feather.

Raider looked sideways at Doc. "Salt Lake, here we come."

"I'm going forward," Doc replied.

"The girl again?"

Doc called Raider into the caboose, where he could speak to him alone. The big man leaned over for an earful. Doc was always figuring things and then telling him about it.

"Raider, I believe that Susanna's father may be having financial troubles."

Raider shrugged. "So? You worried about the agency getting cheated out of the fee?"

"It's not that. Look at the logic of this entire situation. Purchasing a horse to sponsor a winner-take-all challenge race. It's the act of a vain or a desperate man."

Raider's brow was wrinkled. "I see what you mean. It does seem like a crap shoot. But hell, Doc, we ain't s'posed to do nothin' but deliver this horse to Carson City."

Doc sighed. "And she's such a nice young woman. She—"

"Jesus God Almighty, Doc!"

The track swelled on a rising grade. The engine was starting up the steep slope, straining to pull the rest of the train. A loud, metallic cry resounded from between the cars. Raider hung in the doorway of the caboose. Doc was right behind him.

The livestock car broke away, rolling back down the incline. Raider was out of the caboose before Doc could blink. His broad frame sailed between the cars. Raider's hands grabbed the railing of the livestock car. He clung there a yard away from the narrow doorway.

Doc yelled back, but Raider didn't hear him. "I'll stop the train and come back for you."

Doc grabbed the handholds of the ladder on the side of the caboose. He swung over onto the top and balanced himself. As he started for the engine, the livestock car disappeared behind him, rolling backward toward the station at Green River.

Doc fired a round from his .38 Diamondback, shooting into the dark sky. "Stop the train!"

The engineer looked back at him, wondering if he was about to be robbed. Another man was standing next to the engineer, holding a coal shovel in his hands. He recognized Doc.

"That's the Pinkerton."

The engineer looked back up the slope. "I can't stop it now. We'd have to brake all the way back down. It would take us thirty minutes."

Doc gestured with his pistol. "Then do it! Now!"

The engineer growled under his breath, "Your boss is gonna hear about this. All right, let's see if we can get ourselves killed."

"Hurry," Doc said, "before my partner beats us to it."

Raider clung to the cascading boxcar, saying a prayer that he had learned in Sunday school when he was a little boy. He could hear Judith and Eastern Star in the livestock compartment, braying and whinnying, probably as scared as he was. A small voice came behind the animal sounds.

"Save me, Sweet Jesus!"

Freeman was quivering inside the boxcar.

"Hang on, Zeb," Raider cried.

He swung his legs over to the small girder on the front of the car. Doc had once showed him how to hand-brake a railcar. He saw the spoked wheel on the end of the iron rod. Just turn it, Doc had said. Just turn it.

Raider's hands closed over the spoked wheel. He strained

until the iron circle began to turn. Nothing. Even after he had tightened it down about halfway. He kept spinning the wheel, repeating the prayer over and over in his brain.

The car slowed a little as it swung back into the valley. Raider felt more play in the wheel. As the station came back on them, the car slammed to an abrupt stop. Something had been put on the tracks to stop a runaway car. The bogus railman had been a setup.

Raider eased through the doorway, into the car. "You still with us, Freeman?"

A rifle barked outside the car, shattering the boards to the left of Raider's head. He dropped down next to Freeman and stuck his Colt out of the space between the slats. Two rounds hit nothing. The rifle chattered again.

"We've got to move," Raider said, grabbing Freeman's arm.

The black man hesitated. "Where you goin'?"

"They want Star," Raider replied. "If we go back there with him, they won't shoot at us."

Freeman scrambled behind him, crawling on all fours through the livestock car. The rifle continued to pepper the front of the car. Raider came up next to Eastern Star. The stallion had a spooky look in his brown eyes.

"He's scared," Freeman said.

Raider slid over next to the side door. He cracked it a little and listened to the night sounds. A scuffling of feet to his right. The Colt streamed fire, sending an unseen body to the ground. A voice echoed out of the shadows around the station.

"Give up that pony, Pinkerton. You're liable to get your ass shot off if you don't."

Raider howled back. "Shoot us and you kill the horse. We're right next to him."

Raider was sure he heard a muffled argument. As he strained to listen, a pinprick explosion filled the car. A body staggered toward them, falling flat into the hay. As he fell, Raider fired the Colt, jolting him a second time. Freeman's squirrel rifle had caught him the first round. Right in the forehead.

Freeman's trembling hands reloaded the single-shot weapon. "I never killed a man before. I never . . . he was just there. . . ."

"You're doin' a good job of coverin' me," Raider said.

He started to reload his Peacemaker. More feet shuffled

outside. He heard them running in the hard dirt. Raider stood up, spinning the cylinder of the Colt. Freeman was looking up at him.

"I guess I ain't so lucky after all, Mr. Raider."

Raider peered out into the dimness of Green River. "Get ready for them. There's gonna be—"

Raider heard the blast of a train whistle. The rifles started to bark again, only this time they were firing on the engine of the St. Paul-Pacific. Gunfire from the train answered the volleys from the station. Raider stuck out his Colt and joined the melee. A man fell under the car, clutching the hole in his chest.

The livestock car jerked as the train backed into it. Raider ran to the front in time to see Doc and the conductor jumping down to fix the connection between cars. He hung out of the front doorway and fired at the station, covering them as they worked. Slugs kicked up the railroad gravel around the tracks.

"Will it hold?" Doc cried.

The conductor was shaking his head. Doc waved to the engineer. The train jumped forward almost immediately, taking the livestock car with it. Doc and the conductor swung into the caboose. Raider waited until the gunmen gave up before he slipped between the cars.

"Railman was a confidence job," he said to Doc.

"We're out of it," Doc replied. "Let's just hope the cars stay together on the slope."

Raider laughed nervously. "Let's sure as hell hope they do."

The incline grew steeper as the tracks ran into the mountains. Doc and Raider watched as the livestock car creaked behind them. Raider's eyes bulged suddenly.

"The brake. I left it on."

He jumped across to the livestock car, maniacally turning the iron wheel. The iron connection below made an oily sound. Steel hands locked up and held as the train rolled over the mountainside.

Doc tipped back his derby. "We'll want to stop at the first sign of a telegraph line."

Raider squinted at his partner. "Why?"

"I want to wire our employer and tell him that we would like reinforcements, possibly three or four more agents to back us up in Carson City. I want to be on record as saying that there's more to this case than we have been led to believe. I also think the railroad should know about the ambush attempt."

"You gonna try to get more out of the girl?" Raider asked.

Doc shook his head. "Not yet, Raider. Not until I absolutely have to. Do you understand?"

"Yeah," was Raider's only reply.

CHAPTER SEVEN

The St. Paul-Pacific chugged into Reno, Nevada, at 9:55 A.M., a day and a half behind schedule. Doc had hoped to find a telegraph key at the small station, but the nearest line was five miles southeast of Elko. If Doc wanted to send a message to the home office, he would have to alter his route to Carson City.

When the wagon and Judith were unloaded, Doc opened up a compartment in his Studebaker, searching for a map of the area. Raider stood next to him, peering south, scratching his head. He wondered why no one had ever put down a stretch of track between Carson City and Elko. It was only twenty-five miles to the southwest.

Raider looked over his partner's shoulder. "Why ain't there no railroad between here and Carson City, Doc?"

Doc gestured to one section of his map, drawing his finger along a broken red line. "Carson City is served by this railway coming up from the south. Here's another, from California, coming in from the west."

"How come you took this northern route?" Raider asked.

"Quicker," Doc replied. "Even with the ride to Carson City."

As he pored over the map, Susanna Bolton led Eastern Star off the ramp attached to the livestock car. The chestnut thoroughbred wore a bright red blanket that covered most of his body like a sweater. Raider had to smile.

"Look at that, Doc. That namby-pamby horse got on his nightshirt. Uh-oh, female approaching. And Freeman is with her."

Doc ignored Miss Bolton, sticking to his map. She looked up at Raider's sly smirk. He expected her to bad-mouth him, but instead she smiled right back at him.

"Lovely day, isn't it, Raider?"

Raider's body tilted away from her. "Er, I reckon, ma'am. Yes, I reckon it is a fine day."

Susanna glanced at Doc's back. "Good morning, Mr. Weatherbee."

"Here," Doc cried. "I've figured it out. Gather around, quickly. I want you to have a look at the map."

Doc traced his route for all of them, offering the itinerary for group approval. Since the telegraph wires were on rugged ground, Doc would take Freeman and make the detour to send his messages. Raider and Susanna would purchase mounts in Elko and keep Star with them. Doc planned to request backup Pinkerton support in Carson City. They would rendezvous farther down the trail.

Raider ran his hand over his head, smoothing down his hair under the Stetson. "Doc, why we got to split up?"

Doc met Freeman's eyes. "We can't take Eastern Star along this terrain. He has to stay on the established trail. Am I right, sir?"

Freeman thought about it and nodded. "Star shouldn't be walkin' on bad roads or open territory. It could ruin him for the race."

"Why can't we get a wagon to pull him in?" Susanna offered.

"He needs to walk some, Miss Bolton," Freeman replied. "But I don't want to leave him, Mr. Weatherbee. Why do you want me to come with you?"

Doc raised his hands. "You're the only one who can assist me with the telegraph. Since we can't take Star along, Raider must stay with him. And Miss Bolton is not qualified to . . . help me."

Raider wasn't wild about spending any time alone with Susanna Bolton. She was wearing her man's outfit, complete with that obnoxious little hat. Why the hell was she smiling at him?

"Mr. Weatherbee," Susanna said in a chilly voice, "I think you have a wonderful plan there. We'll get along fine, won't we, Raider?"

She hooked her arm through the big man's elbow. He pulled away instantly. Doc wasn't paying attention. He nodded to Freeman.

"I won't ask you to leave Eastern Star, Mr. Freeman. But if you would volunteer, I'd appreciate your assistance."

Freeman cocked his head. "How long am I gonna be gone from Star?"

"No more than two hours at the most. We'll rendezvous here. You see the route?" His finger rested on the map.

"Doc," Raider said, "are you sure you have to send this message now?"

Doc's eyes had a funny glow. "Remember the attack on the boxcar?" he asked.

Sometimes Raider had a good memory for things. "You're right, Doc, the quicker we can get reinforcements, the longer we go on livin'."

"All right," Freeman replied. "I'll go. But before we leave, I got to tell you a few things about Star."

Raider stepped next to Star, running his hand over the animal's shiny red-gold coat. "I know a little bit about horses."

"Not like this one," Freeman replied. "He's special. You got to treat him like a king."

"Boy howdy," Raider said. "Ain't it somethin'?"

Susanna Bolton tilted her pretty head. "What's something?"

Raider patted the red horse blanket. "Aw, I'm just tryin' to remember when somebody treated me as good as this horse."

Doc smiled wryly. "Angelica, Raider. What about her?"

"Oh yeah." Raider was grinning broadly.

Susanna Bolton blushed under the brim of her leather hat. She didn't seem at all impressed with Raider's memory.

As Raider's roan gelding plodded slowly along the dirt trail, he tried to remember everything that Zeb Freeman had told him about Eastern Star. His task was made doubly difficult by the presence of the young woman behind him. The roan was the only mount for sale at the Reno livery. Raider had to ride tandem with Susanna Bolton, with Eastern Star in tow behind them.

"Can't we go any faster?" the girl asked.

Raider shook his head. "Freeman told me walk him most of the way. We don't want him to bruise hisself."

Susanna huffed disgustedly. "I'll bet you love this."

"You was the one slippin' your arm through mine," Raider replied. "And that shit don't make Doc jealous one bit."

"I don't feel safe with you."

Raider laughed. "Hell, lady, that's why most women like me, 'cause they don't feel safe with me."

Her tongue must have had ice on it. "I can't imagine women finding you attractive. You are rather a common sort. I can't imagine—"

"You can't imagine none of the things I done in my life," Raider snorted. "Hell, a prairie chicken like you don't even catch my eye. And you got your nose too high in the air to notice me."

He couldn't see her face, but he thought he was probably pouting in silence. Raider liked it that way. They rode on for a half mile before she disappointed him by talking again.

"Are you saying that you don't find me attractive, Raider?"

Her smallish breasts dug into his back. She tightened her arms around his waist, rubbing her face on his shoulder. Raider reined the gelding and leapt out of the saddle.

"What are you doing?" Susanna cried.

He plucked her from the saddle, holding her away from him like a trapped skunk. She kicked and flailed, but Raider didn't even feel it. He carried her over to Eastern Star and plopped her down on the animal's broad back.

"Are you crazy?" she cried, grabbing the horse blanket.

Star snorted a little and struck his hoof on the ground. Raider rubbed the chestnut's muzzle, settling him down after a few minutes. Then he glared up at the trembling young lady.

"Now you sit there and be real still, sugar."

"I hate you, Raider."

He put a finger to his lips. "Shh, don't act afraid. If you're scared, you might spook ole Star."

"Wait until I tell Freeman about this! Not to mention my father."

Raider chuckled as he climbed back into the saddle of the roan. He figured he wasn't hurting the thoroughbred by putting Susanna on him. She didn't weigh any more than Freeman. It was a good way to cool her down and get her off the roan at the same time. Raider had to admit that she was a pretty little thing. Just wipe that lip-rouge off and strip her out of those rancher's duds . . . He decided not to think about it.

The roan shifted into a walk when Raider urged it forward. He could hear Susanna cussing him under her breath. He thought it was funny until he saw the shapes on the trail ahead of them.

Susanna frowned at him. "Why are you stopping?"

"Don't make no difference," Raider replied. "They already seen us."

"They?"

Raider started forward again, his hand sliding down next to his Colt.

"What do you think you're doing?" Susanna said through clenched teeth.

"Shut up, woman. Don't do nothin' stupid. Nothin' that'll get us killed. I think they're Shoshone. Last I heard they was friendly. I sure as hell can't tell you what they're doin' down this far."

They continued slowly toward the Indians, who seemed to be sitting in the middle of the trail. Raider counted ten. What the hell were Shoshone doing in Nevada? When they turned to look at him, Raider saw that they were kneeling over the carcass of a mule deer. Six of them had rifles. Raider halted the gelding on the trail and waited for one of them to move.

Doc Weatherbee teetered on a telegraph pole, splicing a wire into the copper-based line going north. Below, in the Studebaker wagon, Zeb Freeman watched the telegraph key, waiting for it to move like Doc had said it would. Freeman could not understand Doc's detour. It seemed like a waste of time.

Doc called to him from the pole. "Just keep watching, Mr. Freeman. You're saving me a great deal of time. Now, if you'll just throw the switch the way I showed you."

When Freeman flipped the switch, the telegraph key rattled once. Freeman waved and Doc came down the pole. He hurried to the key and started to bang out his message. "Key operator to key operator. Acknowledge." In less than a minute he had a reply. "Key operator, Cheyenne, ready."

"Good, I'll have no trouble getting through to Chicago. Cheyenne has a very efficient wire office, probably because of the forts nearby."

Freeman was squinting over the batteries that powered Doc's telegraph. "I still can't see why we didn't send these messages from Carson City."

"Mr. Freeman, I am concerned for the safety of Miss Bolton and for the safety of Mr. Bolton's investment in Eastern Star." The telegraph rattled, prompting Doc to send his message to Wagner in the home office. "Train attack foiled. Station not secured, Green River. Request additional officers, Carson City. Await directive."

When the message was sent, Doc turned to Freeman. "I think it is time we had a talk, sir. I want to warn you that your life may be threatened by future circumstances. The attack at Green River will most likely happen again, since someone obviously does not want Eastern Star to run in the stakes race."

Freeman looked saddened. "You tellin' me to get out, Mr. Weatherbee?"

"No. I'm just telling you that we're going into the middle of something. My instincts necessitated this detour. If I send my message from here, a messenger boy in the telegraph office does not gossip about the Pinkerton detective who is operating in town. And, since there is no Pinkerton office in Carson City, my request for support is logical *before* we ride into a hornet's nest. If you'll just bear—"

The telegraph key started to click. Doc picked up a pencil to decipher the code. "Complete mission. Two agents to Carson City in two days. Caution. Expect state cooperation."

Doc examined the last part of the message. Did they mean state government cooperation? Why would the home office expect Doc to need the state authorities? He returned a message. "What are you sending us into?"

After a half hour, the reply came: "Nothing unfamiliar to you or the other one."

"What do they mean by that?" Freeman asked. He read the message over Doc's shoulder.

"You don't want to know," Doc replied.

He could see why Allan Pinkerton had entrusted him with the girl and the horse. Doc was careful and resourceful. He'd weed a narrow path into Carson City, and he'd be able to deal with whatever he found there. Even if he did have Raider along to complicate things.

Doc sighed and shook his head. "What is it that Raider always says? Con-sarned, chicken-picken' jobs."

Freeman laughed. "You sounded just like him."

"'This doth bode a foul eruption to our state.', Hamlet. We're charging into something, Mr. Freeman. Are you ready for a rough ride down a rocky river?"

The black man rubbed his chin, staring at the ground. "I'm just an old colored man that wants to ride a good horse before I die. Big Derby came when I was hurt, and nobody wanted to chance me after." His eyes were glassy as they scrutinized Doc. "Can you keep me from gettin' killed, Mr. Weatherbee? Can you promise me that?"

"I'll do my best, Zeb. But I offer no guarantees. You know the atmosphere of a stakes race. You'll have to risk it like the rest of us."

Freeman folded his hands together, as if he were praying. "I want to ride Eastern Star, Mr. Weatherbee. I don't care if it is mighty dangerous."

Doc extended his open palm. Freeman clasped hands for a hearty shake. The black man laughed.

"Damn you, Pinkerton, gonna get me killed!"

Doc felt a chill down his spine. "We'd better hurry. I want to meet Raider as soon as possible."

Freeman gazed toward the flat, arid horizon. "Yeah, Raider. I wonder how he's doin' with Miss Susanna."

The ten Shoshone braves were frozen around the fallen deer. Raider hesitated with his gun hand. All of them were on foot, although the oldest man held the tether of a white stallion that was damned near as big as Eastern Star. The chief came forward, bringing the stallion with him. Star snorted and raised his front feet, sending Susanna Bolton seat first onto the trail.

Raider gripped Star's tether, trying to hold him down.

"Good horse!" exclaimed the Shoshone chief.

"If you savvy, get your pony away from mine."

The chief grinned. "I savvy plenty." He clapped his hands, and one of his braves stepped forward to take the white horse. The chief then leaned down to offer Susanna a hand. "You fell off, woman."

He picked her up, hoisted her in his arms for a moment, and then plopped her down on Eastern Star. Raider thought the chief was pretty strong for an old man. He wondered how much muscle the chief intended to use.

"Good horse. Are you going to the race? We are going there." The old man kept looking at Star and then at the white stallion. Sizing them up. "Good horse. I will trade you my horse for your horse." It was almost a command.

Sweat diamonds rolled off Raider's forehead, falling into his mustache. Ten braves who wanted to trade. They were off the reservation, but it didn't matter. The three rifles chortled as levers went back and forth.

"Ten to one," Raider said. "They gonna do whatever they please. And we can't really say no."

Susanna was holding on to Star's mane. "What do you mean?"

"We've got to give them Eastern Star."

"No!" Susanna cried. "I won't allow it."

Raider had his eye on the chief. "Tell *him* that, lady. Tell his nine boys that you don't want to trade."

"Can't you just shoot them?"

"Not so loud," Raider said hoarsely.

Susanna glared at the chief. "Who are you, anyway?"

The old man had a toothless smile. "I am Gray Wolf."

"Well, Gray Wolf, I am afraid I cannot trade Eastern Star for your horse. Although your animal does have a nice form."

She was carrying on like she was in charge of the world. The Shoshone elder walked in a complete circle around them. He was smiling, almost like he respected her.

"Good horse. We trade."

"No, I tell you!" Susanna insisted.

The chief looked up at Raider. "She your woman?"

Raider shrugged. "Yeah."

"I am not!" Susanna cried.

The chief put his hands together. "Our horses will run. If your horse wins, you keep woman and horse. If mine wins, I get everything."

"Sounds fair," Raider said.

Susanna was almost hysterical. "Are you insane, Raider?"

He stepped out of the saddle and strode back to the thoroughbred. Susanna jumped down and swung at him with her fist. Raider grabbed her arms and steered her away from the chief.

"Listen to me, woman, that old man can do us like he wants out here. Now he's give us a way out, to save his pride in front of his sons. So you're just gonna have to ride Star."

Susanna gasped. "Me?"

"I'll take off that blanket. You just hang on. Star can take that Indian pony if you just—"

She slapped him.

"Hey, little lady, that ain't no way to be. Now, I promised Doc that I'd be good to you, but you're pushin' me."

"I cannot ride Eastern Star."

Raider threw his hands in the air. "Then give him to Gray Wolf."

Susanna looked at the smiling chief. "I have ridden before." Her green eyes were doubtful. Raider patted her on the shoulder.

"You got the spirit, girl."

Raider stripped off the horse blanket and turned to the chief. "How about runnin' on that stretch yonder?" Raider pointed toward a deep acre of dried grass. The chief nodded in agreement.

Raider measured out the course for him. "Down to the edge and back? How's that, Gray Wolf?"

The chief turned to the muscular brave who sat on the back of the white stallion. Raider gave the course again in sign language. The brave nodded. Raider grabbed Susanna and whisked her onto Star's back.

He handed her the tether to use as a rein. "Susanna, honey, this old boy knows what to do. You just keep him next to that Indian pony and he'll do the rest. You got to hang on, honey."

Gray Wolf pulled both horses together and clapped his hands.

The white pony broke immediately for the opposite side of the grass meadow. Eastern Star lurched behind him, trailing by five or six yards. Raider's throat was dry as he watched Star chasing the white stallion. He had decided to shoot the braves with the rifles if Star lost. If he pulled it off, he'd only have four braves to fight by hand.

He couldn't take all ten of them. It was impossible.

The white pony reached the edge of the meadow and started back for the trail. Star swung wider, still behind. Raider couldn't even see Susanna on Star's back. His hand slid down to the Colt.

The chief was laughing, watching as his pony neared the imaginary finish line. A clear win. An easy win. The braves with the rifles moved up. Then Star came out of nowhere to pass the white horse by a neck. The smile vanished from the chief's face. And Susanna Bolton was still clinging for dear life to the golden mane of Eastern Star.

"Nobody can beat this horse!" Raider cried. He turned to face the chief, whose head was hung in shame. "Clear on out of here, Gray Wolf. And take that pony with you."

The old man backed away, taking his braves with him. They even left the deer carcass behind. Raider hurried toward the chestnut racer, grabbing the stunned girl who rested on his back. He kissed her on the cheek.

"I had my eyes open the whole time, Raider."

He hugged her. "Ole Gray Wolf messed with us, but we messed with him right back."

She gazed up into his black eyes. "It was wonderful," she said dreamily. "He was so fast. And the way he caught the white horse at the end."

Raider took off his Stetson and dried his forehead with his sleeve. "It looked pretty from where I stood. Come on, we better get out of here."

Susanna grabbed his forearm. "Raider?"

"Yeah."

"What if . . . what if I'm not trying to make Doc jealous? What if I really want you?"

Her eyes closed, and she leaned against him, puckered face upturned. Raider wheeled her around and gave her a slap on the buttocks. Her pursed mouth twisted into a snarl.

"I'm going to tell my father about this," she said.

Raider laughed. "Go ahead. I'll just deny it. I'm going to deny all of this, especially the race with old Gray Wolf there. See if you can get somebody to believe you by yourself."

"I'm going to tell!"

"You want Freeman hearin' how you abused that horse?"

She hit him in the chest with her fist. "You made me do that. I was against it from the start!"

"You still rode the horse," Raider offered. "Not me."

She turned away from him. "Stop it. Just stop it. I'm confused."

"Aw, you just miss your boyfriend. Let's go see Doc Weatherbee."

Doc looked up as Susanna and Raider approached his campfire. It was almost dark. He had been waiting for two hours. When he saw Susanna, he immediately went to his wagon for a blanket. Freeman hurried toward Eastern Star. He lifted the thoroughbred's left foreleg.

"This horse has been run," Freeman said.

Doc glared at Raider. "Something happened, didn't it?"

Susanna Bolton was snuggling in close to Doc with the blanket wrapped around her shoulders. Raider threw Star's tether to Freeman. He dropped both legs over the saddle and bounced onto the ground.

Doc bristled at his partner. "What happened on the trail, Raider? Why were you late?"

Raider whirled around and pointed his finger at Susanna. "Ask the lady what happened, Doc."

Doc looked at her tired face. "I'm not sure I want to know. Susanna?"

Susanna put her hand on Doc's cheek. "Nothing bad happened," she said. "Your partner just saved our necks."

Doc was skeptical. "Really? Are you sure he didn't get you into trouble and then simply get you out of the mess he started?"

Raider cut Doc some slack. He smiled. "Ole Weatherbee's got a lot of faith in me."

Doc knelt down by the fire. Susanna slid next to him. Raider warmed his hands, staring into the darkening sky. Doc sure seemed edgy. Maybe it was just the woman. Or maybe he knew something Raider didn't.

Raider leaned down over the fire. "When we goin' into town, Doc?"

"After dark." Doc was staring into the flames. "Raider, two more agents will be joining us shortly."

Raider nodded. "Good." Then his eyes narrowed. "Wait a minute, Doc. You mean they're sendin' four of us just to protect this animal?"

Doc ignored the question. He stood up and peered into the sky. "I want everyone to be careful when we go into town. I don't want to attract undue attention."

Raider didn't like the tone of his partner's voice. "Whoa, Weatherbee. Do you know somethin' that I oughta know?"

"Nothing specific. Just a warning from the home office to be more cautious."

Raider's stomach growled. "Sounds like they're droppin' us into the hot grease again."

The gentleman from Boston was checking the ammunition in his .38 Diamondback. As he dropped the pistol back into his coat pocket, Susanna Bolton moved away from him. Her face was ghostly pale.

"We should talk first," she said.

"No," Doc replied. "We'll talk when Eastern Star is safely inside his stall. Is that understood?"

No one protested.

A cold plains wind disturbed the flames of the fire. Raider cast his eyes to the south, toward Carson City. Freeman was feeding Star next to Doc's wagon. Raider felt bristling hair on the back of his neck. Sitting on top of the Studebaker was the black cat, framed against a dark blue sky. He had come out of nowhere.

"I thought we lost that mangy critter," Raider said.

Suddenly he didn't feel eager about visiting Carson City.

CHAPTER EIGHT

"Looks like we're clear," Raider said.

Zeb Freeman was closing the door of the Carson City Livery and Blacksmith. They had slipped into town virtually unnoticed, procuring a stall for Eastern Star. The only person to take heed of their entrance was a young stable boy, who slid out the back door and ran toward the saloon across the street.

Doc held the reins of Eastern Star, waiting for the burly blacksmith to shovel out the stall where the thoroughbred would rest for the night. Susanna Bolton stood next to the man from Boston, gazing up at the star on the horse's forehead. Her expression was an exhausted frown.

"Freeman," she said. "Does Star look tired to you?"

Freeman patted Star's neck, looking into the animal's eyes. "He's all right. He needed to work some. Got too lazy on that train ride. We don't want him gettin' fat before the race."

Raider tipped back his Stetson and nodded. "No, sir, we don't want him gettin' too tired either. Hey, smithy, is that stall ready yet?"

The smith, a brutish, hairy man, stepped out into the light of several oil lamps. "Ready as it will ever be, partner. You want me to bed him down for the night?"

Freeman shook his head. "No, sir, we'll take care of him."

The smith sighed. "Damn me, I'll be glad when this race is over. I ain't had a minute's rest since this thing kicked up."

Doc handed the smith a ten-dollar gold piece. "Thank you, sir. If we need your assistance, where may we find you?"

"Across the street, over the saloon," the smith replied. "That's where I sleep."

Freeman led Star into the cleaned stall. As the smith made his exit, Freeman started to groom the chestnut stallion. Susanna moved closer to watch him.

Doc turned to his partner. "I'll stay with Star tonight, Raider," he said. "You can find us two rooms in the hotel."

Susanna looked over her shoulder at Doc. "Nonsense, Mr. Weatherbee. You can stay at our house. I'm sure my father will be glad to . . ."

Raider wheeled around toward the stable door, his hand dropping to his Colt. "What the hell is that?"

A commotion had arisen outside the livery. Doc slid his hand into his coat pocket, gripping the butt of the Diamondback. Voices clamored in the street, growing in number with each passing second.

"I'll secure the door," Doc said.

He dropped a plank into the iron cleats on the stable door. Raider grabbed a barrel, wheeling it beside a high window. He stood up and peered out into a mob of fifty men.

"I wonder what the hell they want?"

Doc raised his Diamondback. "Are they angry?"

Raider shook his head. "They just look drunk to me. Wait a minute, there's somebody pushin' through the crowd. A man in a white suit."

Doc pressed his ear to the wooden door. A calm, persuasive voice rose above the others. The man must have been standing against the door. Doc could hear everything he was saying.

"Gentlemen," the man said loudly. "Where are your manners? Are you trying to bring the sheriff down on you?"

A voice challenged him from the mob. "Somebody said that fancy horse is here. The one from back east."

Another man: "Said you got twenty-five Pinkertons guardin' him."

"How can you know that?" replied the calm gentleman. "I don't even know myself, and I'm the sponsor of this race."

Doc looked at Susanna. "I thought your father was behind this endeavor?"

Susanna came up next to the door. "He is. What's going on here?"

The calm voice again: "Look here, all of you. I assure you that—"

From the mob: "We want to see Eastern Star."

"And you will. But you must be patient."

"Are you tryin' somethin' funny, Hilliard?"

"No, in fact, to show my gratitude for your interest, I'm buying drinks for everyone at the saloon. Unless, of course, you don't want a free watering hole for the rest of the night."

"That oughta change their minds," Raider said.

Sure enough, the drunken crowd could not resist the offer of free whiskey. They started away, slowly at first and then in a mad dash for elbow room at the bar. Raider hopped down off the barrel. Doc listened to the knocking at the stable door.

"They called him Hilliard," Doc said to Susanna. "Do you know him?"

"No," she replied.

Doc nodded at his partner. "I'm going to let him in. Stay back and be ready. Freeman, are you all right?"

"Yes, I am, Mr. Weatherbee."

Doc swung open the stable door. Standing in the street were the man in white and two men in dark suits. A large man held a Winchester; the other one, quite a bit smaller, did not seem to be armed. They hesitated when they saw Doc's hand full of the Diamondback.

The man in white smiled. "I assure you, sir, there is no need for that weapon." He stepped into the stable. "Allow me to introduce myself. I am Dalton Hilliard, steward and grand marshal of the Comstock Stakes."

Even in the dim light, Hilliard's handsome presence was disarming. A smooth, chiseled face, penetrating blue eyes, sandy hair. He was almost as tall as Raider, but thin and dapper. He extended an uncallused hand to Doc.

"You must be Doc Weatherbee. We've been expecting you. I trust you had a safe journey."

Doc shook his hand, surprised at the wiry strength. Raider was leaning back against a bale of hay, keeping his eyes on the big man with the rifle. Susanna was glaring at the man in the white suit.

"Who are you?" she demanded. "And where is my father?"

Hilliard smiled with thin lips. "Jacob is resting, Miss Bolton . . . if that is your name. He has been rather tired lately, what with all of the confusion brought on by the Comstock Stakes."

Susanna raised an eyebrow. "What are you talking about?"

"Oh, yes, forgive me," Hilliard replied. "You couldn't have known. We just decided on the title last week. You see, in honor of the twentieth anniversary of the Comstock Lode, we've decided to call the race the Comstock Stakes."

"We?" Susanna challenged.

"Your father and I," Hilliard replied.

Susanna leaned in toward Doc. "I've never seen these men before in my life, Mr. Weatherbee."

Hilliard laughed. "How could you have seen us? Your father just hired me last month. Didn't he mention my name when he was in Kentucky to see you?"

"No," Susanna replied. "I want to see my father right away. Doc, will you take me to my home?"

"Your father is staying in my rooms here in town," Hilliard replied quickly. "The strain has been very great on him. I have been keeping a close eye on him. Luckily I have been able to shoulder much of the burden involved in organizing this—"

"Take me to him now!" Susanna cried.

Hilliard gestured toward the street. "By all means. Shall we go?"

Doc turned to his partner. "Stay here with Freeman, Raider. I'll accompany Miss Bolton and Mr. Hilliard."

"Sure thing, Doc, if you—"

The big man with the rifle slid around Hilliard. "We're stayin' with the horse. Both of you Pinkertons can go along with—"

Raider came out of the shadows. "Somebody die and make you boss, partner?"

The big man glared at Hilliard. "He can't talk to me like that. Even if he is a Pinkerton."

"You was the one who started barkin' orders," Raider said.

Everyone was frozen for a tense moment. The small man

moved in behind the man with the rifle. His hand was in his coat pocket. Probably had a small pistol, Raider thought.

Hilliard stepped between them. "Now, now," he said suavely, "there's no need for bickering. Perhaps some introductions are in order. Mr. Weatherbee, Mr. Raider, these are my two assistants, Frank Teal and Jimmy Jones."

Teal was the big man, Jones the slight one.

Hilliard persisted with his smiling countenance. "Now that we all know each other, maybe we can all be friends."

"I can do without a handshake," Teal said.

"Fine by me," Raider replied. "I'm stayin' here with this colt, Mr. Hilliard. You can just—"

The Winchester lever made a squeaking sound. Raider's hand came up with the .45. Doc and Hilliard put a quick end to the scuffle, but Teal still glared at the tall man from Arkansas.

"You and me, Pinkerton. Toe to toe."

"Time and place, gopher-face," Raider replied.

"Gentlemen, please," Hilliard said. "There's a lady present. Mr. Weatherbee, I appeal to your sense of propriety and obvious breeding. As your employer, Mr. Bolton wishes to see you both immediately. I assure you, Frank and Jimmy will be more than adequate in guarding Eastern Star. If you will just follow me."

Doc hesitated until Susanna Bolton slid her arm through his.

"Please, Doc. I want to see my father."

Doc turned to his partner. "Very well. Raider . . ."

"All right, Doc," replied the big man. "But I ain't sure these two boys can do the job."

Teal bristled. "Maybe one day you'll get to find out how good I am, Pinkerton."

Raider smiled. "Ole buddy, that's one invitation I ain't gonna turn down. You just be ready when it happens."

Doc urged Raider toward the street. "That's enough, Raider. Mr. Hilliard, shall we go?"

They started off down the dirty street, leaving Hilliard's two men to close the stable door behind them.

Jacob Bolton looked as tired as any man could be, Raider thought. He sure didn't cut the figure of a rich gold miner. Gray temples, receding hairline, a lined, sagging face. He was just an inch or two taller than his daughter. When he wrapped his arms around Susanna, his brown eyes were close to tears.

"Thank you, gentlemen," Bolton said in a low voice. "Thank you so much for bringing my daughter to me."

Raider smiled. "Anytime, Mr. Bolton."

There were standing in an office with Dalton Hilliard's name on the wooden door. The room had been decorated like a den, almost like a town house on Washington Square, Doc thought. An interesting touch of New York City in Nevada. Doc was smiling.

"Mr. Bolton, my partner and I would very much like to have a word with you alone."

Bolton seemed irritated. "If you have anything to discuss, please talk to Mr. Hilliard. He's my manager now. I wish to spend some time with my daughter. If you gentlemen will excuse us . . ."

Susanna looked at Doc with her green eyes. "Thank you, thank you so much for everything, Mr. Weatherbee. You too, Raider. I'll see both of you again when my father and I have spent some time together."

Doc bowed to her. "We will be at your disposal, Miss Bolton. You have but to request our services."

Susanna smiled and took her father's arm, leading him through a side door in the study. When they were gone, Hilliard turned to the two Pinkerton agents. In the light from gas lamps, his handsome face was unreadable.

"Have a seat, gentlemen," he said. "Would you care for some brandy?"

"No thank you," Doc said. "Perhaps Raider would."

"No," Raider replied. "Maybe I ought to be gettin' back to the stable."

Hilliard frowned. "You seem to have little faith in my men."

"Star is our responsibility until somebody says different," Raider scowled.

"I'm saying different now," Hilliard replied.

He slid behind a small desk, gesturing toward the padded chairs that sat in front of him. Doc and Raider filled the chairs, hats in hand. Hilliard produced a bottle of brandy, pouring a glass for himself.

"Sure you won't join me?" he asked.

Doc shook his head. "We aren't supposed to drink on duty."

Hilliard shrugged. "Ah, don't worry, I won't tell anyone. Relax, you just came in off the trail. You need some time away from—"

"Mr. Hilliard," Doc said, "we have been hired by Miss Bolton to oversee the security of Eastern Star. She is our employer, along with her father. If you wish to have us dismissed from the assignment . . ."

"Easy, Mr. Weatherbee," Hilliard broke in. "No one said anything about dismissing you. I just thought you might like to rest before you—"

"We don't rest until the job is done," Raider offered.

Hilliard nodded. "I'm sure that's true. And if I can help you in any way, please feel free to ask."

Doc leaned forward a little. "Then you wouldn't mind answering a few questions for me?"

Hilliard hesitated and then replied, "Ask away."

"Is Jacob Bolton having financial trouble?" Doc asked quickly.

Hilliard forced a grin. "No, of course not. Business has never been better. One of the reasons he hired me as manager was to help him with his affairs. If it's . . . oh, I see, you're worried about your fee. Well, worry no more, Mr. Weatherbee. I'll have your expenses for you first thing in the morning. If you will just give me a total . . ."

"Four hundred dollars for the trip out here," Doc replied. "The private cars were expensive."

Hilliard's eyes narrowed. "Four hundred. Does that include your fee?"

"Yes, up until our arrival here in Carson City."

"Then I'll have a bank check for you in the—"

"You may wire the money to the home office," Doc replied.

"Very well," Hilliard said. "Anything else?"

Doc leaned back in the chair. "When we were coming up the street to your quarters here, I noticed that the offices of the Bolton Mining Company were closed."

"Surely," Hilliard replied. "It is the middle of the night, after all."

Doc nodded. "But you see, the lettering for the company insignia was scraped off, leaving only the impression of—"

"We're putting up new lettering." Hilliard threw back the glass of brandy and poured another one. "You know, Mr. Weatherbee, if I weren't an educated man, I'd take offense at your inquiries. It's almost as if you don't trust me."

Doc laughed. "On the contrary, I'm only looking out for the interests of—"

"Susanna Bolton?" Hilliard said with a self-satisfied smirk on his face. "Yes, I saw the way she looked at you. Perhaps I should remind you that she is a very impressionable young woman. Don't get any ideas about overstepping your boundaries, Mr. Weatherbee. You are a hired man, after all."

Raider was surprised that Doc just sat there and took it from Hilliard. The big man from Arkansas didn't really like the smooth man's uppity tone. But Doc seemed as calm as a deep river.

"I assure you," replied the man from Harvard, "that my association with Miss Bolton is strictly professional. If you are an educated man, Mr. Hilliard, you should see that immediately."

"My apologies, Mr. Weatherbee."

"No offense taken."

Raider shifted in his chair. "Before you two start clappin' each other on the back, I think me and Doc oughta be gettin' back to the livery. I don't want nothin' happenin' to that two-thousand-dollar pony."

"No hurry," Hilliard replied. "Have you eaten dinner?"

Raider exhaled, shaking his head. "I'm confused about somethin', Mr. Hilliard. We was hired to protect Eastern Star. Now there's already been one attack on that horse . . ."

"My God!" Hilliard exclaimed. "When did this happen?"

"Green River, Wyoming," Doc replied.

Hilliard downed the second glass of brandy. "Thank God you made it through without losing the horse."

"Thank *us*," Raider said.

"How could such a thing happen? My word, these western states are uncivilized."

Doc leaned forward. "So you see, Mr. Hilliard, it is very important that Raider and I remain with Eastern Star. Someone does not want him to run in the Comstock Stakes."

Hilliard mused for a moment and then smiled. "Well, I think

the worst is over. And I have two men guarding Star right now. I don't think you and your partner should concern yourselves tonight. Go to the hotel and have a good night's rest. You can start fresh in the morning."

Raider scowled. "I ain't one to chase a hen around the henhouse tryin' to get her to drop an egg, Mr. Hilliard. Now you tell us straight. Are we on this job or not?"

Hilliard's blue eyes went right through him. "I'd say that's up to Mr. Bolton, my large friend. And he doesn't want to be disturbed right now. So, if you will—"

Someone knocked on the door of Hilliard's office. At his command the door swung open and the man known as Jimmy Jones strode into the room. Raider saw the look on Doc's face when the small man entered. Recognition. The light in the study was brighter than the dim glow of the stable.

"Jimmy Boy," Hilliard said. "Perhaps you can convince our two Pinkerton friends that Eastern Star is safe."

Jones smiled, revealing a gold front tooth. "He's safe all right. And I took that darkie over to the hotel. Didn't even want to take him in till I told them he was your manservant. They's makin' him sleep in the back. Here's keys to your rooms."

He threw the keys on Hilliard's desk. Hilliard picked them up and offered them to Doc. "Now, will you accept our hospitality?"

Raider grimaced. "This a load of horse—"

"Fine," Doc said. "Raider, I believe Mr. Hilliard is right. We could use a night's sleep. And since Mr. Jones has gone to all this trouble, we would be rude not to take the rooms."

Hilliard smiled. "I knew you would see it my way."

Doc rose and shook Hilliard's outstretched hand. Raider looked at his partner as if he thought Doc was loco. Surely Doc wasn't going to let Hilliard's men guard that prize racehorse.

"Hold on, Weatherbee," he said. "Are you sure you want to—"

Doc started for the door. "Give it a rest, Raider. We can talk to Mr. Bolton in the morning. I'd just as soon we were off this case anyway. I'm rather bored with the whole thing. Good night, Mr. Hilliard."

"You're a good man, Mr. Weatherbee," Hilliard replied. "I'm glad you see that there's no need for alarm."

"Quite. Raider, are you coming?"

"Hellfire, Doc, I reckon I am."

Raider was scratching his head as he rose to follow his partner out into the street. Doc could sure change directions in a hurry. And then it occurred to him that Doc might be onto something.

Raider stopped his partner when they emerged out of Hilliard's storefront on the edge of town. "Doc, did you mean it when you said you were wantin' off this case?"

"Of course not," Doc replied. "Let's get away from here before we talk any more. I don't want to be overheard."

They found a dingy cantina where a Mexican girl served Raider a cup of steaming coffee. Doc lit up a cigar, expecting his partner to protest. But Raider only glared at him through the vapor from the coffee cup.

"What's goin' on in your head, Doc? It ain't like you to come into a cheap hole like this. Couldn't we talk back at the hotel?"

Doc's brow wrinkled. "In rooms procured for us by Dalton Hilliard? I hardly think so."

Raider leaned back in the wooden chair. "All right, Yankee man. I know you're about to put the kettle on the fire. Let's hear what you're cookin'."

Doc blew out a puff of smoke into the rancid air of the cantina. "From the beginning. First, if you will recall, Susanna Bolton told us that her father was against her hiring Pinkerton detectives to help transport Eastern Star."

"Yeah. So what?"

"Did you notice Hilliard's reaction to the figure that I gave him for our expenses?"

Raider nodded. "Yeah, for somebody who says business is good, he sure as hell flinched when you totaled it up."

"Furthermore," Doc continued, "the offices of the Bolton Mining Company were vacant when we passed by. They're changing the insignia for another company that's going in there."

Raider's eyes were narrow. "Are you sure?"

"I can corroborate the evidence in the morning."

Raider spooned sugar into his cup. "Hell, Doc, it ain't no crime to go out of business. If ole Bolton there is havin' trouble with his money . . ."

"Then why would he hire a manager and two other men?" Doc offered. "Wouldn't he want to conserve his resources? And why would he sponsor a race like the Comstock Stakes?"

Raider dropped the spoon. "You're confusin' me, Doc. One minute you say Bolton is hurtin' for a buck, the next breath you're tellin' me that he wouldn't be doin' all this if he was broke."

Doc tilted his head. "No, but I am telling you that he might be operating under the coercion of another party. Someone who has told him that he will resurrect his failing business."

"Hilliard," Raider said.

"Precisely."

Raider looked skeptical. "I don't know, Doc. We ain't got much to feed on. Besides, nobody could arrest Bolton for taking a business partner."

"Just hear me out. I agree that probably nothing illegal has taken place—yet. But there are a few things that remain to be seen. I'd like to keep an eye on Hilliard. If he wires our expense money to the home office, we will have reason to believe he is legitimate. However, if he fails to forward the money, we will know that he is not the kind of man who pays his bills."

Raider shrugged. "Maybe so. Boy, I'd hate to be him if he tries to cheat ole Pinkerton out of a red cent."

Doc raised his finger. "Another thing. Did you see his reaction to our news of the attack at Green River?"

"He was kinda shocked, if you ask me."

"An overt reaction. Too overt. And then he brushed it off as if it didn't mean a thing. Up and down too quickly. Almost as if . . ."

Raider frowned. "Like he knowed about it beforehand."

Doc nodded.

Raider slammed his cup on the table. "Hell, why would Hilliard attack his own train? What would he have to gain by stealing his own horse?"

"Bolton's horse," Doc replied. "And I don't know. But I do intend to poke around first thing in the morning."

Raider eyed the man from the East. "I'm goin' back to that

stable tonight, Doc. I don't care what Hilliard says."

"Stay out of sight if you do."

Raider snorted. "I can take that Teal boy the best day he ever lived. And that Jones boy . . ."

"His name is not Jones," Doc said. "His name is Johnson. Jimmy Boy Johnson."

"I thought you recognized him. Is there a story to go with it?"

Doc stubbed out his stogie. "Remember last year, when you had to go down to Yuma to testify when you got that innocent man out of prison?"

"Yeah, I ain't forgot."

"I took the opportunity to travel east," Doc said. "I visited New York, Providence, and Boston. While I was there, a delicious scandal was brewing in New York. A man named Johnson was barred from the racetrack at Belmont. He was involved with a steward named Wagonner. They were fixing races, or at least trying. When they were discovered, Johnson was barred from racing for the rest of his life."

"What about the other boy, what'd you call him?"

"A steward," Doc replied. "Like a judge. He oversees the running and the fairness of the race."

"What happened to him?"

Doc shook his head. "No one knows. He simply disappeared, right before Johnson was ousted. There were no images of him to print in the newspaper. Johnson wasn't so lucky. His portrait was all over the front pages of every journal in the city. As soon as I heard Hilliard call him 'Jimmy Boy,' I knew he was the man. The face wouldn't have been enough, not right away. But the name brought it all back to me."

Raider shook his head. "I don't know, Doc. That all sounds a little farfetched to me. I mean, this Johnson showin' up here ain't no real surprise. He was bound to come out here after he was kicked out of the East. Unless . . . unless Hilliard is that steward. But even then . . . I don't know."

Doc pointed his finger in the air. "The fact remains that Hilliard did not want us staying with Eastern Star tonight. He even forced our friend Freeman out of the stable. He must be up to something."

Raider drained the coffee cup and stood up. "Come on,

Doc, let's go see how ole Freeman's makin' out at the hotel."

"Very well," Doc replied. "Remember, when you go back to the stable, stay outside. Don't let anyone see you."

"You know me, Doc. I'm sneakier than a otter in a gator's nest."

"I'm sure you are," Doc replied. "Whatever that means."

When they were outside, they saw a boy nailing up a large poster. It was an invitation for all comers to enter the Comstock Stakes. "BIG HORSE RACE NEXT SATURDAY. All horses welcome. $100 to enter. $10,000 in gold for the winner. Betting on winners only. Apply, Dalton Hilliard, 27 Main Street. Gold prize in strongbox with Wells Fargo. Challenge the great horse from Kentucky, the thoroughbred, Eastern Star."

"There you go, Doc," Raider said. "The money's over at the Wells Fargo office. It's on the level."

The boy looked up at Raider. "Gonna be hundreds comin' to try that horse. Gonna be just like a circus, like the county fair."

The kid ran off down the street, carrying his posters under his arm.

"He's right," Raider said. "How's anyone gonna cheat all of them people that's comin'? Hell, they'd never get away with it. As far as I can see, Doc, this thing's gonna be over on Saturday."

"Possibly," Doc replied. "And then again, it might just be getting under way."

CHAPTER NINE

Raider shifted in a half sleep, waking every time a noise caught his attention. He had been sitting behind the stable most of the night, watching the rear entrance. If Hilliard was up to something, he would be sneaking in the back way, even in darkness. So Raider waited, dozing in restless intervals, rousing out of his nap at the slightest sound—the cry of a drunk cowboy, a rattling harness, a rat scurrying along a wooden wall, the rinky-tink chatter of an untuned saloon piano. He listened until Carson City was fast asleep, until the soft plodding of unshod hooves snapped him to his feet.

As the man approached with the horse, Raider peered up toward the sky. Somewhere between midnight and dawn, he thought. He glanced back at the figure that approached the rear entrance to the stable. The horse snorted in the cool air. It seemed to be white, but it was hard to tell. A creaking from the rusty hinge. The shadowed wrangler led the horse into the dim stable.

Raider drew his Colt and started to lean out of the alley where he had been hiding. Something snapped to his left. More footsteps in the dark. He stepped back into the alley. A second man strode toward the stable. Raider would have recognized the white suit in a blizzard. The hinge creaked again as Dalton Hilliard entered the stable.

Raider thumbed back the hammer of the Colt. "Looks like we're havin' ourselves a little tea party."

He sorted out his options. He could just bust in on them, waving the Colt, demanding an explanation for their clandestine activities. Or he could go get Doc—but that might allow them to escape. He had to wait, to see if they did something with Eastern Star.

Hilliard and the other man were damned quiet in the stable. Raider slipped up next to the door, listening. Muffled voices were inaudible. What the hell was Hilliard planning? Footsteps coming for the door. Raider jumped into the shadows. Hilliard came out of the stable, calling to the other man as he left.

"Just make sure no one can tell the difference," Hilliard said.

"You gonna pay me?" asked the man in the stable.

"When the job is done. Lock this door behind me."

Hilliard closed the stable door and started away. Raider waited .for him to turn the corner around a wooden building. Then he moved along the wall, back to the stable door. No more voices from inside. Teal was probably sleeping with his rifle. Raider peeked through a crack in the door, but he could only see blurred shapes in the poorly lighted barn.

"Damn it all," he muttered under his breath.

He wished Doc was there. Doc would know what to do. If he left to go get him, the man in the stable might be gone before they got back. Raider stepped away from the wall, gazing up to see if a loft door might be open. Everything was locked up tight. He'd just have to wait to see if the man came out before morning. If he barged in uninvited, he might get a taste of Teal's Winchester.

Back to the alley, sliding against the damp wall. Raider sat down on the bottom of an overturned rain barrel. The Colt felt heavy, so he holstered it. His eyes closed gradually until he was sleeping. A rattling and the creaking door roused him.

When he opened his eyes the morning light blinded him for a second. Someone shut the stable door. Raider leaned around the corner to see a tall man in a brown serape. The man stretched his arms to the sky, yawning. His hat was worn low, so Raider could barely see his dirty, grizzled face. The man looked at his hands when he was through stretching. Raider rubbed his eyes. The man's hands looked pitch black.

Suddenly the man glanced up. "Who's there?"

Raider reeled out of the alley, swaying as if he were drunk. "Shay, par'ner, gimme a silver dollar for a bottle."

"Damn rummy," the man said. "Get away from me."

Raider staggered back down the alley, toward the hotel. When he turned the corner, he broke into a run, bolting through the hotel lobby, up the stairs. Doc had already risen and was dressed for the day. He sat on the edge of his bed, listening to his partner.

"And you say they brought in a white horse?" Doc asked.

Raider nodded. "Yep."

"Well," Doc replied, "at least Star is in his stall."

Raider ran a hand over his wavy hair. "Doc, they ain't gonna let us back in that stable. Hilliard and that black-handed boy are up to somethin'."

Doc's brow wrinkled. "Black-handed?"

"Yeah, it seemed funny to me, too. That boy that came in with the horse had hands as black as the ace of spades. Does that make sense to you?"

Doc shrugged. "Not yet. But I'm sure it will in time. Raider, you get some sleep. I'm going to find out what I can about Bolton and Hilliard."

Raider wasn't smiling. "You think Susanna's daddy is deep in all of this?"

"I certainly hope not," Doc replied. "Although we haven't seen any evidence to the contrary."

"No, we ain't."

Raider didn't like the look on his partner's face. Doc was thinking about the green-eyed lady too much. Even a smart man like Doc could go crazy over a woman. And that wasn't the kind of man Raider wanted to back him up in a tight spot. Especially if it came down to facing Teal's Winchester.

Doc Weatherbee was elated. The morning's activities could not have gone any smoother. With each step he had taken he had come closer to answers about the state of affairs concerning

Jacob Bolton's mining interests. The citizenry of Carson City had been more than willing to talk about Jacob Bolton and the young dandy named Dalton Hilliard. Nearly all of the community "pillars" were unhappy about the impending horse race. Such an event lessened the stature of a place that boasted a government mint within the city limits.

Doc hurried up the wooden sidewalk toward the hotel. He cast a sidelong glance at the livery where Frank Teal had denied him entrance earlier in the day. No one was to be admitted without written permission from Dalton Hilliard. Doc had to smile. He couldn't wait to tell Raider what he had learned.

The big man was pulling on his boots when Doc rapped on the door of his hotel room. "Jesus, Doc, you're smiling like a raccoon eatin' a cucumber sideways. Ever'thing all right?"

Doc took off his derby. "Are you ready to listen? Because I've learned a great deal since this morning."

"Hell, Doc, let it fly."

"All right. First, Jacob Bolton is—"

They both looked toward the window. A woman's piercing cry echoed through the street. Raider shook his head.

"What now?"

Doc's face was perturbed. The woman screamed again—a long, sharp wailing. Other voices rose in the street.

"Think we ought to go, Doc?"

The man from Boston slipped on his derby. "Let's have a look."

"We could leave it to the sheriff," Raider replied.

"No. It could be related to the matters at hand. We'll have time for talk afterward."

Doc stomped out with Raider right behind him. They hurried through the lobby, into the street. A buckboard wagon rattled down the middle of the dusty thoroughfare. Bodies were stacked high in the bed of the wagon, like neat piles of cordwood.

Raider pulled down the brim of his Stetson. "Somebody's been busy."

"Let's have a closer look," Doc rejoined.

A crowd was gathering around the wagon, making it difficult for Doc and Raider to get near the bodies. Women were fainting while their wide-eyed children shinnied up wooden posts to get a better look. Suddenly the crowd parted, allowing a chubby man to come through them. He wore a tin star on his vest. The sheriff, Raider thought, a soft one, the kind of lawman who wasn't used to big trouble.

The sheriff clenched his teeth when he saw the bodies. "Clear out, all of you. Go on." He drew his Remington .38 and fired a shot into the air. "I said git!"

Most of them obeyed him. Doc and Raider moved closer as the mob dispersed. The sheriff ignored them as he rolled off one of the dead men. The corpse hit the ground with a dull thud.

"Gray Wolf!" Raider said.

The sheriff spun around and glared at him. "Who the hell are you, mister?"

"Name's Raider, Sheriff. This is my partner, Doc. We're Pinkerton operatives, just blew into town last night. Brung in that racehorse."

"Pinkertons, huh?" He rubbed his fat belly. "You knowed this Injun?"

He nudged the body of Gray Wolf with his foot.

Raider nodded. "Ran into him on the trail. Had nine others with him. Looks like they got 'em all."

The sheriff scowled at him. "They? You know who killed them?"

Doc leaned in toward the portly lawman. "Sheriff, perhaps we should talk in your office. You see, we were hired to protect Eastern Star. Are you familiar with the Comstock Stakes?"

"Familiar?" the sheriff said. "Hell, I ain't had nothin' but trouble since that damned race come up. I'd put a stop to the whole thing if that damned Hilliard didn't have a special paper from the state legislature. He must have his nose up pretty far to get somethin' like that."

"No doubt," Doc replied.

The sheriff glanced back down at the body of Gray Wolf. "Poor bastard. I wonder what the hell he was doin' this far south? This ain't Shoshone country."

"Had a horse with him when I saw him last," Raider replied. "Said he was comin' here to the big race. Guess he ain't gonna make it."

The sheriff looked up at the driver of the buckboard. "You see a horse near these men?"

"No, sir," the driver replied. "But I didn't find them. Territorial marshal hired me to bring them here. Said he didn't have time to do it. I reckon he was the one what found them."

The sheriff emptied his lungs. "Damn it." He looked at Raider. "You know why anybody would want to kill these Shoshone?"

"No, sir. Unless they wanted that white horse."

"All right," the sheriff said. "Get 'em over to the undertaker. I guess he'll plant anybody what's dead."

The buckboard rattled down the street, flanked by the onlookers along the sidewalk. With surprising quickness the sheriff pivoted on his heels and started in the opposite direction. Doc and Raider went after him.

"Sheriff," "Doc said, "I think you should be aware of the complications that may arise from this horse race."

The sheriff stopped and turned toward Doc. "Look here, Mr. Pinkerton, my job is to protect the citizens of this town. Now, I can't do nothin' about that race, so it's out of my hands. Until then, I'm arrestin' anybody what breaks the law, includin' both of you. So if you got business here, then you take care of it without botherin' me."

Raider raised his hands. "What if somebody does somethin' illegal?"

"Then you come and find me as quick as you can," the sheriff replied. "I'll put the chains on 'em and run 'em under the jailhouse. Otherwise, I don't want to see hide nor hair of either of you."

He waddled off toward his office. Raider shook his head. "That's a troubled man, Doc."

"I agree. But I believe it would be better if he stayed out of our way. He'll be there when we need him."

"Yeah, I reckon. Damn it all, Doc, that's a shame about that Injun. I wonder how somebody got the drop on all ten of them?"

Doc was peering toward the hotel. "I wouldn't even venture a guess, Raider. But I would like to tell you what I learned this morning. Perhaps it will all tie in when we have the complete picture."

"Hell, let's get goin'. I want you to tell me before you bust."

They started along the street, stepping up on the wooden

sidewalk. Doc hesitated when he heard his name being called from behind him. Freeman was running down the middle of the street like the devil was after him. Raider caught him when he stumbled onto the sidewalk.

"Mr. Weatherbee, Mr. Raider, he's gone!"

Raider squinted at the black man. "What are you talkin' about?"

"I sneaked into the stable just now," Freeman replied. "I crawled into the back of the hay wagon and hid where nobody could see me."

Doc put his hand on Freeman's shoulder. "Easy, sir, just tell me what you saw."

"Star's gone," Freeman gasped. "He ain't in his stall. He ain't nowhere in that livery."

"He can't be gone!" Raider cried. "I watched that place all night. And if they took him out during the day, ever'body would have seen them. There woulda been a big commotion all over town."

Freeman raised his right hand. "I swear before God that horse ain't in his stall."

Raider looked at his partner. "How could they get him out of there without nobody seein', Doc?"

"I'm not sure," Doc replied. "They've even closed the livery for day-to-day business. We could talk to the blacksmith."

Freeman shook his head. "I heard the hay driver talkin'. Said the smith is over to Silver Springs to shoe a draught horse. Said he won't be back till Friday."

Raider lifted the Colt from its holster. "Then I'm goin' in there to have a look-see for my ownself."

"Put up your pistol," Doc said. "This is a matter that I want to discuss with Dalton Hilliard."

Raider hesitated and then dropped the Peacemaker into the holster. "All right, Doc. But if he don't have some answers, I'm gonna ask a few questions myself."

"Why, that's the most ridiculous thing I've ever heard," said Dalton Hilliard. "Star isn't missing. He's in his stall where he belongs. I was there just this morning to see him myself."

Hilliard was sitting behind his desk, leaning back in his chair. He wore a dark brown suit that blended into the walls

of the study. Doc and Raider sat opposite Hilliard, balanced
on the edges of their chairs. Raider's gun hand was dangerously
close to the butt of his Peacemaker.

"Freeman says Star ain't there, Hilliard."

Hilliard's blue eyes fell on the big man. "Mr. Raider, I'm
surprised at you. A man from south of the Mason-Dixon line
ought to know better than to believe a ni—"

"The color of his skin is not pertinent," Doc interjected.
"He says that Eastern Star is not in his stall, therefore I am
inclined to believe him. You should believe him too, since he
is training Mr. Bolton's horse and he also intends to ride him
in the Comstock Stakes. Unless Mr. Bolton has changed his
mind about Freeman."

Hilliard leaned forward. "I assure you, Freeman is our rider."

Raider scowled at the man behind the desk. "You seem to
do a lot of assurin', Hilliard. How about assurin' us that horse
is in the livery?"

Hilliard shrugged. "You have my word, gentlemen. Isn't
that good enough for you?"

"We'd like to see Eastern Star for ourselves," Doc replied.
"And I would also like to talk to Jacob Bolton myself."

"Er, Mr. Bolton and his daughter have gone to Lake Tahoe
for a few days," Hilliard said. "He and Susanna wanted to
spend some time alone."

"Where are they stayin'?" Raider asked.

Hilliard exhaled impatiently. "Both of you are worried about
nothing, I can assure . . . I'm telling you straight out. Jacob and
his daughter are staying in a little cabin right on the lake. If
you're willing to ride a couple of hours I can tell you exactly
how to get there."

Doc reached for a piece of paper on Hilliard's desk. "Write
down the directions to the cabin for us."

Hilliard stood up. "This is all becoming very tedious, Mr.
Weatherbee. Perhaps I should dismiss you from this assignment
altogether."

Raider pointed a finger at him. "Bolton hired us, and he's
the only one who can fire us. And since he ain't here, then
we're still on the case."

"And we want to see Eastern Star ourselves," Doc rejoined.

Hilliard turned away for a moment, gazing into a wall of

books. When he faced them again, he had an enigmatic smile across his thin mouth. "So you want to see Eastern Star? Very well. In fact, I was planning to put him on display for the entire community tomorrow."

Raider's eyes narrowed. "What are you talkin' about?"

Hilliard laughed. "I knew that would get your attention. You see, I intend to open the center ring of this circus. If you want to see Eastern Star, be at the livery tomorrow at two-thirty in the afternoon. Is that agreeable?"

Doc seemed to be as perplexed as his partner. "All right, Mr. Hilliard. Two-thirty it is. And don't forget to write down the directions to the cabin where Jacob and Susanna are staying."

Hilliard laughed. "Just can't keep away from her, can you, Weatherbee? Well, let me tell you, you haven't a chance there. She'd never look twice at a man like—"

Doc stood up quickly. His fists were balled up and his face was contorted in a hateful fit of rage. Raider thought he was going to take off Hilliard's head right then and there.

"Mr. Hilliard, your personal opinion of me does not matter one whit to me. However, if you are inclined to make another off-color remark about Miss Bolton, I am afraid you may find yourself embroiled in an old-fashioned duel. Is that understood?"

Hilliard's jaw was grinding. "When Mr. Bolton returns, you will be dismissed immediately, Mr. Weatherbee. Until then—"

Doc reached across the desk, grabbing the lapels of Hilliard's coat. "The directions to the cabin, sir. And don't be slow about it."

Hilliard jerked away from him, quickly scrawling something on a sheet of paper. Doc snatched it from his hand when he was finished. Raider stood up next to his partner. He was kind of proud about the way Doc had handled the slick man in the fancy suit.

Doc tipped his derby to Hilliard. "Good day."

Hilliard's thin lips were curled. "Be careful, Mr. Weatherbee. You should know how precarious a town can be when the citizens are caught up in a stakes race."

Doc smiled. "Yes, I remember last year, when a steward and a jockey were dismissed from the racetrack at Belmont. If the bettors had gotten hold of them, there wouldn't have been much left. I suggest you watch your back as well, Mr. Hilliard."

Doc turned and strode out of the study. Raider shot Hilliard a dirty look before he followed his partner. They were halfway down the street when Doc slammed his fist into his palm.

"Raider, I'm sorry I lost my temper back there, but I won't have that man passing remarks about Susanna. She's too fine a lady for that."

Raider nodded. "Yeah, I know. I was glad you gave it to him, though. If anybody's got it comin' . . ."

"No," Doc replied. "My behavior was crass and unprofessional. I'll try to keep a rein on my temper from now on."

"Sure, Doc. What about that cabin? Are we gonna take a look?"

Doc shook his head. "I wouldn't trust Hilliard to tell us the truth. And if we keep an eye on anything, it should be the livery. Although I do hope that Susanna is not in any sort of trouble."

Raider stopped in the middle of the street. "Hey, Doc, you ain't told me about that stuff you found out about this mornin'."

"Wait until we're in a good vantage point to watch the stable," Doc replied. "Then I'll tell you everything."

They settled in on the roof of the hotel, looking down on the stable. Freeman was situated behind the livery in a place where they could see him. He would signal if anything happened. Raider peered down at the closed door of the livery.

"Doc, where the hell is your mule? Didn't you put her and your wagon in the same place?"

Doc nodded. "Judith was there until Hilliard had her moved to another stable. My wagon has been behind the hotel all the time. I didn't want to take any chances."

Raider grunted. "Can't blame you there. Hell, ever'thing seems quiet down there. You think we're barkin' up a empty tree?"

"Something happened to that horse. Freeman could not have been mistaken. He knows Star like his own child."

"Yeah, I reckon." Raider looked at his partner. "You ever gonna tell me about this mornin'?"

Doc sat down on the edge of the roof. "Jacob Bolton is dead broke."

Raider grimaced. "What?"

"Not a penny to his name," Doc replied. "He owes everyone in town. The bank refuses to loan him a cent. I spoke to a surveyor who says that his mines haven't produced a nugget of gold in six months."

Raider shook his head. "Hell, I ain't never heard of a gold miner goin' broke. Where'd he spend it all?"

"Who knows? It really doesn't matter. I suppose he squandered some of it, probably speculating on new mining claims. And he sent his daughter back east. That must have set him back some."

"Yeah," Raider said. "And he bought himself a racehorse."

Doc nodded. "He could have spent his last two thousand dollars on Star. By the way, the home office has not received a remittance from Hilliard. He obviously does not intend to pay."

"So that's why Jacob Bolton didn't want us along for the ride. He couldn't afford to hire the agency."

"Correct," Doc replied. "Only his daughter insisted that Star have protection on the trip west."

Raider looked away from Doc. "I know you don't want to believe she's in on it, Doc, but..."

"Don't say it, Raider."

They were quiet for a while. Raider vented his nervousness by cleaning the Colt. His brow wrinkled as he glanced back at his partner.

"Somethin' I can't figure, Doc. Who was it tried to ambush us back there at Green River?"

Doc's eyes were trained on the stable. "I've been thinking about that. There might be someone else who doesn't want Star to race—his competition, perhaps. Ten thousand dollars in gold is a lot of money. Providing, of course, that the money is indeed in the strongbox at Wells Fargo."

"You think that poster is a lie?"

Doc looked at him. "What do you think?"

Raider snorted. "I think I can't wait until tomorrow afternoon at two-thirty."

When the stable door swung open, the crowd gasped. Hilliard had opened only the top half of the door to keep back the spectators. Doc and Raider leaned against the bottom portion of the aperture, gazing into the dim livery. A chestnut stallion whinnied inside. Frank Teal was holding the horse's tether. The ever-present Winchester rested on Teal's hip.

"My God," said a voice in the crowd. "He must be fourteen hands high."

The others echoed the sentiment. Hilliard was grinning triumphantly. He moved back to Teal, holding his hands over his head. "Quiet, please. You don't want to spook him."

The stallion snorted and struck the ground with his hoof. Freeman stuck his head between Doc and Raider. He saw the unmistakable star on the chestnut's forehead.

"Is it Eastern Star?" Doc asked in a whisper.

"It looks like him," Freeman replied. "But they got him back too far for me to be sure."

Raider tipped back his Stetson. "Ain't no denyin' it. That's Eastern Star, all right. You was wrong, Freeman."

Doc reached for the latch on the inside of the door. "I'm going to take a closer look for myself."

The Winchester was aimed right at him. "Far enough," Teal said. "Ain't nobody comin' in here."

Hilliard stepped forward. "He's right, Mr. Weatherbee. You've seen your horse. Now, if you'll just move along with the rest of the—"

A loud screeching resounded from inside the livery.

"Oh, my God!" cried a woman in the crowd. "Look!"

Doc and Raider peered into the shadows. They both saw it. The black cat was arched on top of the stall, hissing at Eastern Star. Teal swatted at the cat with the barrel of his rifle. A shadow flew down off the stall, disappearing behind a stack of hay.

Hilliard started to close the door in their faces. "You've seen quite enough, gentlemen."

Doc smiled at him. "Yes, Mr. Hilliard, I think we have."

CHAPTER TEN

When Doc returned from dinner in the evening, he found Susanna Bolton waiting for him in his hotel room. She was sitting on his bed, clad in a simple gingham dress. Her pretty face was red from too much crying. She threw her arms around Doc, burying her cheek in his chest, pressing her warm body into his.

"I'm afraid, Doc."

"Shh." He stroked her brown hair. "It's not as bad as all that."

"Yes, it is."

She started to sob. Doc reached into his coat pocket for a handkerchief.

"My father sold our house on the lake. And he hired that man . . ."

"Hilliard?" Doc asked.

She looked up with her red-streaked green eyes. "I don't like that man, Doc. I don't like him at all. He's got some kind of hold on my father. I can't figure out what it is."

There was anger in Doc's voice. "Has he hurt you, Susanna? Has he done anything . . ."

She shook her head. "No. Thank God. Although he's always ... looking at me. And he's made jokes to my father about asking for my hand in marriage."

"I'll do my best to prevent that unfortunate occasion."

Her face was suddenly hopeful. "Doc, I know you can get my father out of this mess. Will you try? Please? I'll retain you. I'll find a way to pay Allan Pinkerton."

Doc smiled reassuringly. "I wouldn't be concerned with such things, Susanna. A Pinkerton man never leaves a case until it is resolved."

She hugged him harder. "I love you, Doc. I really do."

He pushed her away. "Susanna, I've discovered a great deal about your father's finances. It might change your opinion of me if I tell you. Perhaps I should let you know what I've learned."

Susanna turned toward the window, gazing down into the street. She could see the livery where Eastern Star was boarded. A hateful voice came out of her diminutive body.

"Can you tell me worse than I have imagined, Doc? Do you think you can hurt me worse than seeing my father fall so low?"

Doc put his hands on her shoulders. "Susanna, you must do everything you can to help your father."

She turned back to face him, sliding her arms around his waist. "What can I do to help him, Doc?"

"Go back to him," Doc replied. "Stay with him, give him your love and support. Also keep an eye on Hilliard."

Susanna lifted her hands to Doc's face. "I'll go back to my father tomorrow, Doc. Tonight, I'm going to stay with you."

"Susanna!"

She kissed his mouth, wrapping herself around him, pressing her firm breasts against his chest. Doc did not resist her. He returned the kiss, holding her tightly.

Susanna had lost her breath. "Doc, make love to me."

He cupped her nipple in the palm of his hand, rubbing it through the gingham. At the same time, he guided Susanna's hand to his groin. She buckled against him, rubbing the hardness that grew inside his trousers.

Doc kissed her neck and ear. "Are you sure, Susanna?"

"Please."

Doc began to flip the buttons of her dress. Susanna caught on and started to undress him at the same time. When they were naked, Doc saw a moment of hesitation in her eye. He pulled her into his body, driving his shaft between her thighs.

"Don't be ashamed," Doc said.

She looked up innocently into his eyes. "May I turn out the lamp?"

"No," Doc replied. "I want to see your beauty in the light."

She backed away from him, gliding onto the feather mattress of the hotel bed. Doc followed her, parting her legs, guiding his penis into the wetness between her thighs. Susanna trembled when he penetrated her.

Doc found a slow rhythm, slipping his penis in and out of her, bringing a languid frown of pleasure to her face.

"Not inside me, Doc. Please."

"I won't."

Doc felt the rising jism. He waited until the last possible moment before he withdrew from her. Her fingers waded through the sticky emission. Doc lowered his mouth to her sweet lips. He kissed her for a long time before he rolled off her.

Susanna stretched out next to him. Doc stroked her hair, gazing up at the ceiling, wondering if any complications would arise from making love to the lovely young lady. He hated having to send her back to her father and Dalton Hilliard.

"Doc?"

"Yes, my dear?"

She trembled again. "Will my father have to go to prison?"

"I'm not sure, Susanna. Do you think he's going to commit a crime?"

"I don't know, Doc. I just don't know."

"Don't be afraid."

She sat up. "Doc, what if Hilliard finds out that I slipped away to see you? Oh, I've got to get back. If he knows . . ."

Doc reached for his trousers. "You can go out the back way."

"What about the front? What if Hilliard comes into the hotel?"

Doc stepped over to the window, gazing down into the street. "Don't worry, my partner is on the roof. And I daresay, very little gets by him when he's on his toes."

Of course, when Raider wasn't on his toes, it might be cause for worry.

• • •

Raider leaned back in his chair, listening to the footsteps that came up behind him. The footfalls had been slow, almost indecisive. Not a very big person approaching. Raider kept on watching the livery, pretending that he did not notice the clumsy attempt to sneak up on him. His hand closed around the butt of the Peacemaker on his side. In one smooth motion he corkscrewed out of the chair and brought up the .45.

"That's just about far enough."

He could not see a face in the shadows of the rooftop.

"Step over here real slow-like."

A woman's meek voice came out of the darkness. "You do not know me, Señor Raider?"

Raider lowered the Colt. "Who the hell . . ."

Her scent was on the breeze as she stepped toward him. "Remember," she said. "In Reno, a long time ago."

"Lupe?"

"Sí, you know."

Raider shook his head. He had known her long before he went to work for Allan Pinkerton, in a restless time when he had drifted. Lupe had just been one of many women, but he had actually lived with her, almost like husband and wife. He had stayed with her for almost a whole month.

"Lupe, what the hell are you doin' here? And how'd you find me?"

"I work here as a maid in the hotel. I saw you, but I didn't want to bother you. You are an important man now. I hear them talking."

Raider dropped his Colt into the holster. "Aw, I ain't nothin' like that. I'm just helpin' out some folks."

"Raider, they plan to kill you."

He chuckled. "Now how do you know that, Lupe?"

"I hear things."

"Well, thanks for warnin' me. If there's anything I can do for you, just holler."

She grabbed his crotch. "I'm married now."

Raider reached behind her and cupped her buttocks. "Why are you doin' that to me if you're a married woman?"

"He cannot make a child."

She started to unbutton his pants. Raider lifted her dress, rubbing her bare ass. He remembered it being pretty good with

Lupe. She was big-chested and a little plump.

Lupe pushed him back into his wooden chair and climbed into his lap, straddling his body. She guided him into her moist crevice, gasping as he entered. Raider grabbed her ass, lifting and lowering her onto his cock, all the time watching the livery door over the woman's shoulder. There was no reason to neglect his duty just because he was cutting a little.

"You are the biggest," she moaned.

Raider discharged inside her, giving her what she had come for. He felt funny thinking about the possibility that he might make her pregnant. But then he figured she had an old man, so he would take care of everything. Lupe slipped off his lap.

"Goodbye, Raider. I hope nothing happens to you."

"Lupe?"

She turned back to look at him. *"Adiós."*

"You need money or anything."

Lupe crossed herself. "I don't do that now. I am an honest, God-fearing woman. I must go pray now for what we have done."

Raider laughed. "Pray double hard for me, Lupe. I'm an old sinner. Pray that God don't kick my sinnin' ass."

She trod across the roof, disappearing back into the shadows. Raider leaned back in the chair, feeling unexpectedly satisfied. His euphoria abruptly disappeared when he saw Dalton Hilliard coming down the street, heading straight for the stable.

Raider cupped his hands and blew into his thumbs, making the sound of a mourning dove. That was Doc's signal to come up to the roof. Raider watched as Dalton Hilliard entered the livery by himself. Raider signaled again as Doc was walking up behind him.

"What is it?"

"Hilliard's in the stable," Raider replied. "You want to go in."

Doc shook his head. "Not yet. Let's watch for a while."

They stood for a silent half hour, keeping their eyes trained on the front entrance to the livery. Then Raider saw the waving torch behind the stable. He pointed it out to Doc.

"That's Freeman."

Doc nodded. "Is your gun loaded?"

"I'm ready for bear."

Doc started toward the stairs. "Then let's join our friend Freeman."

They huddled in the shadows, watching the rear entrance to the livery. Raider couldn't stand sitting still. He wanted to move, to find something wrong and set it right. Doc was too damned cautious sometimes.

"Anybody come in or out this way?" Doc asked.

Freeman nodded. "A man in a poncho went in right before I waved the torch."

"That'd be the man I seen," Raider chimed in. "Looks like him and Hilliard is havin' another meetin'."

"I'd love to hear what they're saying," Doc said. "Raider, go back and cover the front. If you see anything . . ."

The stable door creaked. A dark figure came out of the livery, looking in both directions.

There was enough light for Raider to see the poncho. He nudged his partner. "That's the man I saw before, Doc."

A second figure joined the man in the poncho. Dalton Hilliard. He was leading a chestnut horse on a tether. The poncho man slipped back into the livery and brought out a second horse, a big black stallion. He gave the black's rope to the poncho man, who led both horses away from the stable. Hilliard watched for a moment until Teal appeared at his side.

Raider whispered to Doc. "He loves that Winchester, don't he?"

Hilliard strode back into the stable, leaving Teal to close the stable door. When it was shut tight, Doc and Raider came out of the shadows. Freeman was standing right beside them, scratching his head.

"Where was they takin' Star?" Freeman asked.

"Perhaps to the racetrack," Doc replied.

Raider had his hand on his Colt. "What was he doin' with that black?"

"I'm not sure yet," Doc replied. "I want to be certain I know all of the facts before I make a conjecture."

Raider squinted at his partner. "A what?"

"An educated guess."

Freeman struck a match and fired the bowl of his cherry

pipe. "I'm worried, Mr. Weatherbee," he said. "I don't want them to hurt Star. And I'm afraid they ain't gonna let me ride him."

Doc put his hand on Freeman's shoulder. "That's the only thing Hilliard would guarantee, Mr. Freeman. He said you were unquestionably the jockey for Eastern Star."

"You think I should ride him?"

Doc smiled. "By all means, sir. Your riding Eastern Star fits right into my plans."

"You hatched a nest full of eaglets?" Raider asked.

"Let's just say I've feathered the nest," Doc replied.

Raider was peering in the direction where the poncho man had taken the two horses. "Don't you think we ought to follow that other boy, Doc?"

"No, Raider. I'd much rather have a look inside the Carson City Livery. Of course, it would be a good idea to wait until Dalton Hilliard leaves."

Freeman shivered. "Let's hope he takes Teal with him when he goes."

The heel of Raider's boot splintered a rotten plank in the side wall of the livery. Two more kicks widened a hole big enough for passage by a man. Doc slipped through first, with Raider and Freeman behind him. He struck a sulphur match and quickly found a lantern. The stalls were deserted except for one tired gray mare.

Raider had his Colt in hand. "Hurry it up, Doc. See if you can find what you're lookin' for. What the hell are you lookin' for?"

"This," Doc replied.

He held the lantern over two wooden washtubs full of paint. One held black, the other a red-brown hue. Blobs of the thick covering had fallen all over the hay on the stable floor.

Raider laughed sarcastically. "Paint? That's what you're wantin' to find?"

Doc moved away from the tubs, toward the forge where the smith pounded out his shoes. "The furnace is hot. And there: the anvil has been used recently. It's still warm."

Raider's brow was fretted. "I thought the smithy was in Silver Springs."

Doc raised the lantern higher. "What's that at your feet, Raider?"

The big man looked down to see the black cat winding around his boots. "Hellfire, he scares the bejesus out of me."

Doc bent over to pick up the feline friend of Eastern Star. A rifle lever chortled. Raider raised his Colt only to feel a slug creasing his wrist. He dropped the .45 into the hay.

Teal recocked the Winchester. "Get that cat, Jimmy Boy."

The smaller man jumped for the cat, trapping the black fur between his arms. Two sets of claws scraped his face, barely missing his eyes. Jimmy Boy screamed, looking at the blood on his hands.

Teal screamed at the little man. "Damn it, you're lettin' that critter get away!"

A black blur scaled a post to the loft. He was gone in the dark mounds of straw. Teal's doggish face contorted in anger.

"You stupid little son of a bitch! I was against bringin' you along with us. After what you did at Belmont."

Jimmy Boy skulked back away from the bigger man. "Don't worry, Frank, that horse'll run without the cat. I'm givin' you my word."

Teal turned toward Doc and Raider. "I'm gonna kill them."

"You're not going to kill anyone, Frank. Not yet."

Dalton Hilliard, clad in his white suit, sauntered toward his henchmen. He put his hand on Teal's shoulder and smiled. His smile disappeared when he saw Jimmy Boy's cat-scratched face. "Whatever happened to you, Jimmy Boy?"

"He let that cat get away," Teal interjected.

Hilliard motioned toward the Pinkertons. "Get their guns, Jimmy Boy. Make sure you search all of their pockets and their boots."

"I'm wearing overgaiters," Doc said.

Hilliard clapped his hands together. "Bravo, Mr. Weatherbee. A fine jest from a condemned man."

Teal grinned. "I get to kill them, boss?"

"Later," Hilliard replied.

Doc whispered to Raider, "Goad the big one into fighting you."

Raider laughed. "With pleasure, Doc."

Teal took a step toward Raider. "What's so funny, Pinkerton?"

Raider held his injured wrist. "I was hopin' you and me could tangle, Frank. But now you're gonna take the easy way out by killin' me in cold blood. Kinda cowardly, ain't it?"

Teal snarled at him. "I can take you easy, cowboy. You don't want to fight with a bum hand."

Raider kicked dirt at him. "I can take you with one hand, Frank. You look like a fat gob of guts to me."

Teal turned to his boss. "Let me try him, boss."

Hilliard looked amused. "Shall we wager on the fight?"

Doc bowed to Hilliard. "By all means."

"Let's go outside," Raider said. "Bring some torches."

"You got it, Pinkerton," Teal replied. "You can have all of me you can handle.

He tossed the Winchester to Hilliard. The man in the white suit wasn't taking any chances. He ordered Jimmy Boy to bind Doc and Freeman. Then he ushered the entire party out in back of the stable.

Four flaming torches were stuck in the ground to make the boundaries of the fighting ring. Raider took off his shirt, stretching his wounded hand. It was his right. He would have to use his hook, his hardest left hand. Teal was still wearing his coat and hat. He drew a line in the dirt.

"Toe the mark, Pinkerton."

Raider stepped toward the center of the ring. He felt a jolt in the middle of his back. Hilliard had struck him with the butt of the Winchester. Raider staggered right into Teal's fist.

"Round one," Hilliard cried.

Raider fell backward, hitting the ground. Teal rushed him, diving headlong to pin him. The big man rolled to his left and Teal flew onto the torch. He jumped up, patting out the fire on his chest. Raider got up slower, trying to gather his senses.

"Damn you, Pinkerton!"

Teal started to circle around him, like a drooling bear. Raider's black eyes focused finally. Teal came at him with a roundhouse swing that Raider managed to duck. Teal was big, but he was slow.

Raider caught another blow on his right forearm. Then he swung up with his left, a vicious uppercut that caught Teal on the chin. Teal staggered backward, toward his boss.

Hilliard stopped his man and reached for one of the torches. He gave it to Teal to use like a club. Raider retrieved his own torch, squaring off with the ugly bear man.

Teal swung the torch at Raider's midsection. Raider jumped back, letting Teal chase him until he was winded. Then he swung over Teal's head, knocking his felt hat to the ground. Teal dropped the torch and charged him.

Raider hit him on the back with the torch, but it didn't stop Teal. He caught Raider around the waist, tackling him, pushing him into the wall of the stable. Raider's knee came up into Teal's stomach, forcing a grunt from the flabby breadbasket. Teal released his bear hug.

Raider dropped the torch and started swinging with his left. Teal staggered more with each blow, trying to fight back but unable to overcome Raider's trail-hardened strength. He fell face first into the dirt, with the big man from Arkansas standing over him.

"Get up, Teal. Get up if you can."

Doc looked at Dalton Hilliard. "Your man is down. My man wins fair and square. You owe me, sir."

Hilliard raised the barrel of the Winchester. "We never exacted a wager."

"How about our lives in exchange for leaving town?" Doc offered.

"That's more of a bargain," Hilliard said. "How do I know you won't be back? You've been a thorn in my saddle so far."

Doc shrugged. "There's nothing here. Just a horse. You've got your paper from the legislature."

Hilliard smiled. "Very good, Mr. Weatherbee. Can you guess the senator?"

"Either Coombes or Barkum, I'd say."

Hilliard's face slacked into a frown. "You're too smart, Mr. Weatherbee.

He raised the rifle and pointed it at Doc's chest. Raider dived, knocking his partner out of the bullet's flight. Then all hell broke loose. Two more rifles joined the melee from above— only they were trained on Dalton Hilliard. Teal's Winchester shattered into pieces. Hilliard was untouched.

Raider looked up at the roof of the stable. "Ain't many men can shoot like that. Pinkertons?"

"McNeil and Avery," came the reply.

Raider held up his hands. "Toss me a rifle."

A Winchester flew down into his fingers. Raider rattled the lever and pointed the barrel at Dalton Hilliard. "Sit right still, partner. It wouldn't take a hell of alot to make me shoot you. Rusty, P.W., come on down here."

Doc retrieved his weapons from Jimmy Boy and then cut the bonds that constricted Zeb Freeman. "It's about time they arrived. And not a moment too soon."

Rusty McNeil and P.W. Avery climbed down to join their fellow agents. McNeil was tall and lean and dressed like a farmer; P.W. wore a freshly pressed suit that made him look almost as dapper as Doc. They were good men, proficient and fearless. They all shook hands.

Avery tipped his hat to Doc. "Sorry we're late, Mr. Weatherbee."

Raider clapped him on the back. "I'd say you were right on time."

McNeil gestured toward Hilliard with his rifle. "Want me to take him over to the sheriff's office, Doc?"

The man from Boston got up in Hilliard's face. "No. We've only had a little misunderstanding. Haven't we, Dalton?"

Hilliard studied Doc, wondering if he was being baited. He had a cautious smirk on his thin lips. Doc pushed him backward a little.

"Go on, Dalton," he said. "You're free. I'm not going to press charges against you."

Raider couldn't believe what Doc was doing. "He tried to kill us just a minute ago. You can't be settin' him loose."

Doc gave Dalton a hard shove, sending him to the ground. "You didn't try to kill anyone, did you, Mr. Hilliard?"

Hilliard scrambled to his feet, staring at Doc.

"No laws have been broken," Doc continued. "They're simply going to have a race. Am I right, Dalton?"

Hilliard nodded slowly. "I underestimated you, Mr. Weatherbee."

"Yes, you did," Doc said. "Now, if you will be so kind as to leave us alone, Dalton."

Hilliard ran through the alley, turning the corner. Doc turned back toward his compatriots. They were gawking at him as if they could not believe he had freed the man who had wanted to kill him.

"Don't worry," Doc said. "I'm not loco."

Avery shrugged. "You got your reasons for doin' what you did, Doc."

McNeil rested his Winchester on his shoulder. "Of course, you're gonna tell us why you did it, aren't you, Doc?"

Doc shook his head. "I'm not going to tell you, I'm going to show you."

Raider started to wrap a bandage around his gun hand. "Can you tell me when you're gonna let us in on your secret, Doc?"

Doc looked at Freeman. "On race day, partner. On race day."

CHAPTER ELEVEN

People came from all over the territory on Comstock Saturday. They trailed into Carson City, under the white banners that hung over the main avenue declaiming, "First Running of the Comstock Stakes." On Saturday morning the crowd began to circle around the mile and three-quarter makeshift track that Dalton Hilliard's crew had dragged in the soft earth. Four booths had been set up to take bets—win only—from the farmers and sodbusters and drifters that wagered a hard-earned dollar in dreams of glory.

Raider stood in front of the odds board, wondering where to put his money. Eastern Star was installed as the one-to-five favorite, on reputation alone. The rest of the field, twenty-five horses in all, was set at twenty-to-one, except for an entry named Ebony Cat, which stood at fifty-to-one. Raider had seen Star take the Indian pony without even breaking a lather. He just wondered if Star had been upset by all of the commotion and traveling. Sometimes a horse just decided he didn't want to run.

"Who are you bettin' on, Doc?"

The man from Boston was watching the betting booths.

Hilliard had been walking between the shacks, carrying a leather satchel. At the end of the line of booths sat a Concord coach that Hilliard entered from time to time, only to emerge with an empty suitcase. Doc figured there had been a lot of gold and silver wagered on Eastern Star.

He turned to his partner. "Raider, before you squander your back pay, why don't you at least look at the horses."

Raider had his script in hand. "Aw, I want to bet, Doc. It won't take but a second."

"You may not want to gamble when you hear what I have to say."

Doc had that expression on his face, the one he got when he had figured something out and it was all about to come together. Raider followed him through the crowd, moving toward the edge of the track, where the horses paraded up and down."

"There he is," Raider said. "Eastern Star."

Freeman sat on the back of the chestnut, clad in his jockey silks. He was the smallest man in the race, weighing slightly less than Jimmy Boy Jones, who sat atop the black stallion, Ebony Cat. As Freeman passed by Doc and Raider, he nodded. Doc tipped his derby to the diminutive black man.

"What was that all about?" Raider asked.

"Freeman isn't riding Eastern Star," Doc replied.

Raider gawked at him. "The hell you say."

"I knew it when I saw the cat reacting to him in the stable. The cat knew it wasn't Star. Freeman knows too, now that he's been able to get close to him."

Raider had his black eyes trained on the chestnut. "Doc, what the hell are you talking about?"

"Look at Star. The neck is too short, the chest isn't deep enough. Now look at Ebony Cat. That's the real Eastern Star, Raider. He's been painted black, the same way another horse has been painted brown, the horse that is called Eastern Star."

Raider saw the difference in the stallions. He wouldn't have noticed if Doc hadn't pointed it out to him. "No wonder Hilliard didn't want anybody to get close to Star. I wonder where they got a horse that looked so much like . . . the damned Indian pony!"

Doc nodded. "The man in the poncho must have killed Gray

Wolf. It was the easiest way to get a horse big enough to pass for Star. But look at him—he's a whole hand shorter than Star."

Raider glanced around at the crowd of bettors. "These yahoos can't tell the difference, Doc. They ain't seen Star before."

Ebony Cat passed by them. Jimmy Boy Jones leered at Doc from the saddle. Raider could see black paint caked in the horse's tail. It was Eastern Star all right. And the Indian pony was masquerading as the real thing.

Raider's eyes narrowed. "Wait a minute, Doc. Why would Hilliard risk losing a ten-thousand-dollar purse by switchin' horses? What does he have to gain?"

"The betting pool, Raider. All of their money wagered on the fake Star. Ebony Cat, the real Star, will probably win, and Hilliard will only pay off on one winning bet. He gets to keep the rest for himself. I doubt that there is a first prize in gold, but even if there is, Hilliard plans on rewarding it to himself."

Raider looked at Jimmy Boy. "And he's got that cheatin' rider from back east to help him."

A trumpet blasted the call to the starting line. The parade of horses turned away from Doc and Raider. Cheers rose from the crowd. Many of them would remember it as the most exciting event in their lives. Cries of impatient bettors came from the lines in front of the betting booths.

Raider's throat was suddenly dry. "I don't like this, Doc. These people could go wild-asses if they found out the truth."

"Let's hope they don't."

Doc glanced behind him, searching for McNeil and Avery. They were stationed by the first betting booth. "Raider, stay here and watch the race. Grab Jimmy Boy and Ebony Cat as soon as the race is over. I'll send McNeil and Avery to back you up."

"Where are you goin?"

"To detain Hilliard," Doc replied.

He had his Diamondback in hand.

"Be careful in this crowd, Doc. It could get awful nasty."

Doc turned away from him and headed for the Concord coach where Dalton Hilliard had been stashing the receipts from all the wagering.

• • •

When Doc opened the door of the Concord coach, he saw Susanna and her father, sitting bound and gagged on the leather seat. Around them were bags of lucre—a healthy, if illegal, haul for Mr. Hilliard. Doc slid in and closed the door behind him. He slipped the gag out of Susanna's mouth.

"He's planning to leave," she said.

Doc nodded. "I know."

"Help my father, Doc. He doesn't look good."

Jacob Bolton's face was ashen. Sweat poured off the old man's forehead. Doc loosened the gag and the ropes around his hands. Bolton could barely catch his breath.

Susanna put her hand on Doc's shoulder. "We've got to get him out of here."

Doc stared at the old man. "Why, Jacob? Why did you endanger your daughter's life? Why did you get mixed up with a weasel like Hilliard?"

Bolton's hand was on his chest as he wheezed. "Said he would help . . . said I would be rich again . . . did it for Susanna . . . did it for her."

The door of the coach swung open. Hilliard stepped back when he saw Doc's pistol pointing at him. "Get in," Doc said. "We can talk about your little scheme to defraud all the people betting on the Comstock Stakes."

Hilliard hesitated before he stepped up into the coach. Then he smiled at Doc. "I get it. You're looking for your share. I'm sure we can work something out, Mr. Weatherbee."

"Again you underestimate me," Doc replied. "I'm taking you to the sheriff, Hilliard, and if he won't lock you up, I'll take you to the state marshal. Your bribed senator won't get you out of this one."

Doc felt cold iron on his neck. The muzzle of a rifle had come through the window behind him. Hilliard reached over and took away the Diamondback.

"Teal!" Doc muttered.

Hilliard smiled. "Hello, Susanna. Have you told Mr. Weatherbee that we're engaged?"

"We are no such thing! Don't believe him, Doc."

Teal climbed into the coach with them. He glared at Doc. "Want me to kill him, Mr. Hilliard?"

"You'll get your chance for blood," Hilliard replied.

The coach lurched forward, pulled by a team of horses.

Hilliard gestured with the barrel of Doc's .38. "I'm taking you all along with me," he said. "When we're safely away, I won't need you anymore. Except for you, Susanna. I'll always need you, my love."

Susanna spat in his face. Hilliard slapped her hard across the mouth. Teal's Winchester was the only thing that kept Doc from killing Hilliard.

The man in the white suit leaned back on the seat, his blue eyes bulging from his face. "You can kill all of them, Frank. You can kill them when we get to Reno."

Jacob Bolton gasped and fell forward, holding his chest. His face turned a purplish blue, and foam poured from his pale lips. He shook violently for several seconds and then collapsed against the coach door. Doc reached down to feel for a pulse, but he couldn't find it.

"He's sick," Doc said.

"Sick hell," Hilliard replied. "He's dead."

Hilliard opened the door and pushed Susanna's father out. She began to scream hysterically. Doc wrapped her in his arms, trying to keep her from clawing out Hilliard's maniacal eyes. The coach rolled on toward Reno, stirring dust into the hot afternoon air.

When the starter called *Go!*, Eastern Star and Ebony Cat immediately broke away from the pack. Star, the substituted Indian pony, had a twenty-yard lead on the fake black stallion that Raider knew to be the true thoroughbred. Both horses rounded the first turn well ahead of the field.

Ebony Cat came even on the back stretch, nipping at the heels of the Indian pony. The crowd was hollering for Star, where their money was riding. Raider rooted for Ebony Cat. He had fifty bucks on the real Eastern Star. At fifty-to-one, it would pay a fortune.

The painted chestnut opened a two-length lead going into the final turn. Freeman was a hell of a jockey, Raider thought. And he knew the bogus Star had good form; he had seen that when they had raced the first time. Maybe Freeman knew enough to bring home the Indian pony ahead of his colt. Maybe he was just a damned better jockey than Jimmy Boy Jones.

Raider's fists were clenched. "Come on, Ebony Cat."

The roar rose above the racetrack as the two horses came to the head of the home stretch. Freeman was driving the Indian pony with a right-handed whip. Jimmy Boy stung the flank of the real Eastern Star. It was just like the finish of the race in the meadow: the Indian pony hung on until the end, when a flash of painted blackness nipped him at the wire. Raider jumped up off the ground. He started for the betting window until he remembered what Doc had told him to do.

The crowd was silent as Raider pushed through them toward the track. They were stunned by the lightning finish of the fifty-to-one shot. A few men were lining up at the betting booth to collect their winnings. But most of them had simply lost.

Raider ran onto the track and grabbed the reins of Ebony Cat. Jimmy Boy struck at him with the whip until McNeil and Avery stepped up to pull him down out of the saddle. He was hardly big enough to resist two Pinkertons.

Raider started walking toward the judge's stand. Hilliard had hired an old district circuit rider to oversee the race. He was a senile codger, someone who wouldn't catch on to Hilliard's scheme. His gray head bobbed as he looked down at Raider.

"Who are you, boy?"

"I'm a Pinkerton operative, sir," Raider replied. "I've got evidence that this race was fixed, by this man, Jimmy Boy Johnson, and his boss, a man named Dalton Hilliard."

The judge nodded. "That so? Well, we'll have to discuss this."

A portion of the crowd had followed Raider to the reviewing stand. When the rest of the mob saw the gathering, they closed in behind him. If the black was disqualified, they would get their money back for Eastern Star, which was foolish to Raider, since the real Eastern Star had won. He laid it all out for the judge, who listened intently until the big man had finished.

The old man looked down at Jimmy Boy Johnson. "Is this Pinkerton boy tellin' the truth?" the judge asked.

Johnson sneered at him. "He's lyin'. Yonder is the real Eastern Star."

Freeman led the fake entry in front of the judge. "This ain't the horse I raised from a colt. Look close, judge. These two horses have been painted. If you wash down that black, you'll see he's a chestnut. That's my Star, sir. Not this Indian horse."

Raider caught the old man's attention. "He's right, Judge. Eastern Star really won the race after all."

The judge glared at Jimmy Boy. "What'll it be, boy? You gonna tell me the truth, or do I have to let this mob hang you?"

A vengeful roar went up over the angry spectators. They lunged forward, pushing in toward Jimmy Boy. Raider grabbed the jockey and pulled him onto the reviewing stand. He drew his Colt and cocked the hammer, putting the bore on Jimmy Boy's temple.

"I'll be the one to shoot him if he doesn't tell the truth," Raider said. "Fess up, Jimmy."

Johnson was sweating. "Don't do this, Pinkerton. We'll cut you in. You can have more money than you've ever dreamed of."

Raider gritted his teeth. "Tell 'em, or I'll throw you right in the middle. They'll tear you apart, Jimmy Boy."

Johnson looked into the faces of a lynch mob. He begged Raider not to do it. Raider lifted him off the platform with one hand. "Tell 'em, Jimmy."

Johnson's feet dangled over the ground. "All right! Yes, the black horse is really Eastern Star!"

Raider dropped him onto the platform. The crowd cheered, applauding their victory. Some of them started for the betting booths until Raider fired a shot into the air.

"Whoa, the judge ain't ruled yet." He looked at the old man. "What'll it be, Judge?"

The decision was a long time in coming. Finally the gray head tilted up and the judge raised his hand. "Since Eastern Star won the race, all of those who bet on him will be paid."

It was like a homesteader's race when the bettors stormed the booths. Raider stepped down off the platform, shoving Jimmy Boy Johnson in the direction of McNeil and Avery. "Take care of him. I'm going to find Doc. You boys better clear out. Go back into town. You too, Judge."

Avery squinted at Raider. "What's wrong, Arkansas?"

Raider pointed toward the betting booths. "There ain't enough money to pay all of them. They ain't gonna be happy when they find out about it."

The judge stood up. "We'll pay them out of the prize money. It's right there in that strongbox. Wells Fargo."

Without a word, Raider shot the lock off the strongbox. He threw back the top to reveal a stack of dull gray metal: lead instead of gold.

The judge rubbed his chin. "Somebody's got to go after the men what done this."

Raider agreed. "I'm goin', Judge."

"What about the sheriff?"

Raider spun the cylinder of his Colt on his forearm. "The sheriff don't care about this circus. And I been on this case for a long time."

The judge eyed the big man. "I'm trustin' you, Pinkerton."

Raider snorted sarcastically. "Trust me, huh? Well, Judge, that makes me feel tickled all over."

The Concord coach rattled northward, into the dark glow of an impending rainstorm. A broken halter had delayed them for a while, but Hilliard seemed satisfied now that the coach was rolling again. He had lumped his winnings all around him, transferring them slowly to a large suitcase.

Doc had his arm around Susanna's shoulder. She was sleeping. The strain had robbed her of all spirit.

Doc shook his head, watching Hilliard. "A good take, Dalton?"

Teal sucked on a bottle of red-eye. "Shut up, Pinkerton."

Hilliard grabbed the whiskey from Teal's hand and threw it out the window. "You smell like a distillery. I don't want you drunk until we're safely on the train to Reno."

Doc kept after Hilliard. "You must have fifty thousand there. How does it feel to get rich off the hard-earned money of people who couldn't afford to lose?"

Hilliard laughed. "It feels wonderful. And I don't have fifty, I have closer to eighty thousand."

Teal wiped his mouth with the back of his hand. "When do I get my cut, Hilliard?"

"When our friends are dead."

Susanna raised her green eyes toward Hilliard. She had been listening to him, pretending to sleep.

Hilliard smiled at her. "Have you considered my proposal, Susanna?"

Susanna smiled, but Doc knew it wasn't a sweet invitation. "I'll marry you under one condition."

"And what might that be?" Hilliard asked.

"Don't kill Doc."

Hilliard put a finger to his chin. "Interesting. I'm supposed to let my rival for affections live."

Susanna hardened. "It's the only way you can get me."

"Aw, hell," Teal said. "I wanted to kill both of them."

Hilliard put his hands together. "No, Frank. We'll spare Mr. Weatherbee's life. We'll let him go in Wyoming, in the mountains. He'll have a tough time getting out, but it won't matter. Susanna and I will be married, living back east in a rose-covered cottage."

Hilliard was drunk with new wealth. Doc teetered on the edge of his seat, wondering if Susanna had saved him for a fate worse than a bullet from Teal's rifle. At least he would be alive long enough for Raider and the other two agents to try to find him. He just hoped they picked up the trail before it was too late.

CHAPTER TWELVE

Raider stood over the tracks from the Concord coach, where Hilliard's stage had departed for the north. Doc hadn't stopped him. Raider grew angry when he realized that Doc had left both McNeil and Avery to back him because he would need help with the crowd. The man from Boston should have taken some backup for himself.

Raider gazed toward the clouds sweeping down from the north. "They musta got the drop on Doc."

Freeman shuddered. "Do you think they've killed him?"

Raider shook his head and sighed. "I don't know, ole buddy. Maybe he's with them. Maybe he pulled some plan we don't know about, pretendin' to go along with Hilliard."

Freeman put his pipe in his mouth. "Your partner is a smart man, Raider."

"I know he is. But he can still stop a bullet in the wrong place. That's a hazard in our line of work."

Raider turned and started back toward the racetrack. Freeman dogged his steps, trying to keep up with the big man's stride. The lines were long at the betting windows. People were starting to get restless.

"I got to find Hilliard and bring back that money," Raider

said. "If these people don't get paid, they're going to tear the place apart."

"How you gonna catch them?" Freeman asked.

Raider stopped and looked at him. "I'm gonna take a fast horse, Freeman. I'm gonna ride Star."

Freeman bristled. "You will not."

Raider stuck a finger in his face. "Now listen to me, partner. That horse is the only chance I got right now. I need a edge, and Star's it."

"You can't run a thoroughbred over open country."

"He's a horse, Freeman, a horse that got us into a lot of trouble. We rode into this thing on his back, and I'm gonna ride out of here as soon as I can find a western saddle."

"Star won't take a western."

Raider started walking again. Freeman just stood there. "I'm telling you, Star won't take a western."

"He's a horse, Freeman."

The black man watched him walking back toward the reviewing stand. He started slowly in Raider's footprints and then more quickly to catch up again. "Wait, Raider," he called. "At least let me put the saddle on him. I don't want you putting the cinch too tight."

Star was still tied to the reviewing stand. Raider grabbed a saddle off the back of another horse. He tossed the saddle on the ground and looked at Freeman. "Get him ready. I ain't got all day."

The black-dyed stallion skittered a little as Freeman cinched up the western saddle. Raider slipped his boot into the stirrup and climbed onto Star's back. The thoroughbred felt powerful beneath him, ready to run. Raider held a loose grip on the reins.

"Give him his head," Freeman said. "It's better if you run him all out as far as he will go. He'll tell you when he's ready to stop. He's a great horse, Raider, treat him like a friend."

Star bolted forward with just the slightest urging from Raider's legs. Cool air rushed past his face, making him grab his Stetson to keep it on. Raider had never been on a horse like Eastern Star. He drove hard to the north, knowing that all he had to do was hold on. The colt would do the rest.

* * *

Hilliard's coach arrived in plenty of time to catch the east-bound train to Reno. Keeping Doc's Diamondback under an overcoat, Hilliard ushered Doc and Susanna into a private car. He threw them together in a small compartment, turning at the door to laugh.

"Say goodbye to Mr. Weatherbee, Susanna. You won't be seeing him again after today."

He closed the door. Susanna threw her arms around Doc's neck. He hugged her, stroking her hair as she cried.

"He killed my father," Susanna whimpered. "I just said I would marry him to save you, Doc. He's going to let you go."

Doc held her hand. "I wouldn't bet on it."

The whistle sounded, and the steam engine started to chug forward. Doc lowered Susanna onto a leather seat. She peered up at him with her sad green eyes. "What happened, Doc? What did Hilliard do?"

Doc sat down beside her. "He changed horses in midstream."

"What?"

Doc searched for an Old Virginia cheroot in his coat pocket. He was in luck. He found an untouched stogie and three sulphur matches. A last smoke, if Raider and the others weren't quick. He knew Hilliard would never let him leave the train alive, unless it was to take a walk over the edge of a hundred-foot cliff.

"Susanna, I suspect that your father was not entirely guilty of conspiracy with Hilliard. He may have known, but I suspect he was more of helpless pawn in a gambit."

She put her hand on her forehead. "But what did Hilliard get away with? I don't understand."

Doc leaned back. "The first attack at Green River was an attempt to substitute a fake horse for Eastern Star."

"Why?"

"Let me finish. When the attempt did not work, Hilliard had to wait for Star to arrive in Carson City. He hired a man to paint Star black. To disguise him as a horse called Ebony Cat. In turn, he disguised another horse as Eastern Star. Since few people had gotten a good look at Star, he was able to fool the bettors easily. In turn, Hilliard walked off with the betting pool."

Susanna leaned back against him. "Where did they get the other horse?"

He put his arm around her shoulder. "It must have been hard to find an animal that could pass for a thoroughbred. One of Hilliard's associates killed several Indians to get a white horse. Although I am sure they had some kind of mount for the switch in Green River. The Indian pony was a stroke of fate."

She sighed. "My father said he was doing everything for me. It *was* me. I killed him, Doc."

She started crying. Doc held her close to him, fighting the urge to kiss her. She was so weak and vulnerable. The woman he had made love to was no longer there.

"Your father made unfortunate choices," Doc said softly. "But don't blame yourself for his death."

"Kiss me, Doc. Please."

Her mouth was all over his face. Doc was pushing her away from him as the compartment door opened. Hilliard stuck his head into the chamber.

"The lovebirds, at it again," he said. "Have you said your farewells?"

Susanna clung to Doc. "I'm not going with you, Dalton. I'm staying right here with Mr. Weatherbee."

Hilliard opened the door a little wider. Teal stood there with the Winchester. Hilliard held out his hand to the girl.

"Come along, Susanna."

"I'm not going until Doc is set free."

Hilliard grabbed her wrist and jerked her toward him. Doc came up and planted a fist on his cheek. Hilliard stumbled backward into Teal. Doc lunged for the rifle, but caught only the butt in his stomach. He buckled over onto the floor of the compartment.

"That wasn't very smart, Weatherbee," said Hilliard. He was holding his cheek where Doc had punched him. "Teal, when we're in the mountains, throw him off the end of the train."

They left, taking Susanna with them. Doc rolled up, holding his ribs. Nothing felt loose. He plopped down in the leather seat. As he caught his breath, Susanna began to scream.

"Hilliard!" Doc cried. "I'm going to kill you!"

A hand muffled Susanna's shrill cry. The train began to pick up speed, heading east toward the first stop at Hope Junction. Doc slammed his fist into the wall. There was nothing he could do to stop Dalton Hilliard from raping her.

"Goddamn it, Raider, where the hell are you!"

Raider reined the gelding at the poorly painted sign at the crossroads. A jagged piece of wood pointed northwest, declaring "RENO, 15." Another appendage stuck out to the northeast: "HOPE JUNCTION, 5." Raider was off course. He thought he had ridden too far north.

Hope Junction was still close. Maybe he could get out a wire to the home office. Wagner could warn all the rail agents to keep an eye out for Hilliard and the Boltons.

Raider reached down and patted the neck of Eastern Star. The colt had earned his respect. He flew along the ground without tiring. "Get me to Hope Junction, Star."

The stallion shot northeast, taking the right fork in the road. Raider drove him hard, seeing if he could take it. The long legs bounced underneath the big man from Arkansas, carrying him toward the sound of the train's whistle in the distance. Raider hadn't figured on the train stopping in Hope Junction. Maybe Doc was on board.

Eastern Star got him to the station in time to see the train rolling out. It was a good distance ahead of him. He reached down and stroked Star's mane. The stallion pranced sideways, rearing his head.

"I know you got one last sprint left in you, boy. We got to catch that train."

Raider barely nicked him with his spurs. Eastern Star galloped along the tracks, chasing the private car on the end of the train. Rain started to fall from the dark skies overhead. The whistle blew, mixing with the bass sound of thunder.

Star ran harder in the mud, closing the distance between the station and the private car even as the engine started to pick up speed. Raider planned to swing himself over onto the railing on the back of the car.

They were almost there. Raider stretched out his hand, reaching for the iron rail. Star pounded the sloppy ground, easing Raider's outstretched fingers closer and closer.

Raider swung over as the whistle sounded in the twilight. Rain caught him on the face. He reached for the handle on the door of the private car. But then it flew open and he was looking into the face of Frank Teal.

CHAPTER THIRTEEN

Frank Teal hollered and then lunged at Raider, his hands flying straight for the big man's throat. Raider's arm came up, blocking Teal's flight. They struggled for balance on the back of the train, grappling as the wind rushed by them. A hard left hand from Raider caught Teal in the ribs. The ugly man staggered backward.

Raider hooked hard again with his left, sending Teal's body out into the night. There was only the sound of the train. Hilliard's bodyguard was gone. Raider tried the Colt with his gun hand. He had almost fully recovered from Teal's rifle slug. They were even now.

Raider stepped into the boxcar with the Colt in front of him. He hadn't taken three steps when he heard the girl screaming. He slowly cracked a compartment door and peeked in. Dalton Hilliard was stripped to the waist, writhing on top of Susanna Bolton.

The tall man from Arkansas burst into the compartment, pulling Hilliard off the young woman. Raider's fist sent Hilliard flying out into the narrow passageway between compartments. He thumbed back the hammer of the Colt and pointed it at Hilliard's fallen body.

163

"Move a inch, mister, and you'll have a sinkhole between your eyes. You okay, Susanna? Hey girl . . ."

Raider glanced back at her. Susanna's eyes were closed. She didn't seem to be breathing right.

"Hilliard, if you've hurt that girl . . ."

Hilliard's hand was reaching for the cord that triggered the emergency brake. Raider fired the Colt, but not in time. The train screeched into a slide that sent everyone sprawling. As soon as they were stopped, Raider jumped to his feet again. Hilliard was running toward the front of the car. Raider aimed the Colt and fired. Hilliard was no longer there. He had turned to his left, diving off the train.

Raider heard a pounding behind him. "Doc, is that you?"

The compartment door was locked. Raider told Doc to stand back. All he needed to be a locksmith was his Peacemaker. A single .45 slug did the trick. Doc came out holding his ears.

"Bells in your head?" Raider asked.

"Where's Hilliard?"

Raider pointed toward the front of the car. "He went out the side way. I ain't gonna be far behind him."

"No," Doc replied. "I'm going. Do you have that derringer in your boot?"

"Yeah, Doc, but why don't you take my Colt?"

Mr. Weatherbee shook his head. "The derringer will be quite enough. I'll need some sort of torch as well."

Raider peered out into the night. "Awful dark. It's been rainin' too."

"Just go to the engine," Doc replied. "Reassure the engineer that we aren't under attack, and wait here until I return with Hilliard."

"Good luck, partner."

Doc jumped down off the train with the torch burning. He searched for tracks until he saw a set of bootprints leading to the north. The rain had stopped, leaving the ground just wet enough to hold a muddy impression. Doc looked out into the dark wilderness. He could only venture a guess as to the terrain. Probably all flat, with greasewood and sage.

He extinguished the torch and started in the general direction where Hilliard had fled. The derringer was in Doc's pocket, although he had resolved not to use it unless absolutely necessary. Hilliard might give him an excuse to ply his knowledge of fisticuffs, a chance that Doc intended to take.

The wind came down on him from the north, bringing a second barrage of clouds and rain. Lightning flashed veins of white in the distance. Doc needed to find Hilliard before the night became too nasty.

He fired the torch again, briefly surveying the ground. Hilliard's deep prints showed him the right trail. Doc put out the torch again. He did not want Hilliard to see him coming.

Doc continued on for another hundred yards, keeping his ears to the wind. He thought he detected a low, wailing sound. A coyote howling at the storm. No. It was a man.

The sky burst into electric sheets of fire, illuminating the canyon in front of Doc Weatherbee. He ignited the torch again, stepping slowly toward the rim of the canyon. Another bolt of lightning showed him that the crevice was deep. If he had taken ten more steps in the dark, he would have plunged to a certain demise.

Again he heard the wailing voice. It was much closer. Doc walked along the edge of the gorge, holding out the torch. The cry resounded from beneath him. He looked down, but he could not see a thing. Then the lightning flashed and Doc saw Dalton Hilliard—clinging for life to a slippery boulder on the canyon wall.

After Raider had alerted the engineer and the conductor, he hurried back to the private car where Susanna Bolton still slept. Her face was sweating and pale. Raider put a hand on her forehead. The poor girl burned with a high fever.

He pulled a blanket over her and looked around for a bottle of whiskey. He managed to get a couple of swallows of liquor into her. Then he took a long pull off the bottle himself.

"Is she all right?"

The conductor was standing behind him.

Raider shrugged. "She don't look good. Are there any other women on this train?"

The conductor shook his head. "I got ten passengers, all of them men. What do you want a woman for, anyway?"

Raider scowled at him. "Hell, I don't know. Maybe a woman

would know more about this kinda stuff."

The conductor looked over his shoulder. "Mm, she don't look good."

"Get me some cold water," Raider said. "Jesus, I hope nothin' happens to this girl."

"All right, no need to be so touchy. I tell you, if I had knowed this was goin' on on my train, I never would've let that Hilliard boy come aboard."

Susanna stirred, opening her green eyes. She looked up at Raider.

"Shit," Raider whispered, "you done woke her up."

Her dry lips parted. "Doc? Where's Doc?"

Raider touched her hair, thinking he would like to know the answer to that question himself.

Doc climbed down to where Hilliard was hanging. He watched for a moment, his eyes narrowed. "Your luck had to change sooner or later, Dalton."

A breeze swirled over Hilliard's white knuckles. The rain started again. His hold was beginning to slip.

"For God's sake, Weatherbee. Pull me up."

Doc sat down. "Not without assurances."

"Anything!"

The rain was falling harder.

Doc's torch fizzled. Lightning flashed overhead to light Hilliard's desperate face. The man from Boston let him sweat.

"Hilliard, you must promise that you will tell the court that Susanna Bolton did not have anything to do with your swindle at the Comstock Stakes."

Hilliard's voice was full of hatred. "Yes, God yes! Just get me up from here, you bastard Pinkerton!"

Water was puddling under Doc's feet. "You'll also exonerate Freeman of any wrongdoing, providing that he is implicated as the rider of the fake Eastern Star."

Hilliard's cry diminished into a whimper. "Yes, I'll do whatever you say. Please, don't let me fall. Please."

Doc reached down, grabbing the wrist of the dangling Hilliard, who scurried up quickly off the boulder. He leaned against the rocky wall, looking up into the heavens. Doc put the derringer in his chest.

"I'm climbing up first, Dalton. You follow when I give the signal. One wrong move and you're picking two small slugs out of your gut. Is that understood?"

Hilliard nodded. He still had not caught his breath. Doc turned and climbed quickly to the level ground above them. He looked back to see Hilliard struggling to do the same. The man in the white trousers was almost to the rim of the canyon when he faltered.

Doc leaned over in the rain. "Just two more feet."

Hilliard stretched out his hand. "I can't. The earth is giving way. I can't get a clean hold."

Doc wondered if the man below him might be trying one last trick. Hilliard slipped down a little. He climbed back up, his hand reaching toward the black clouds in the sky.

"Help me, Pinkerton. Help me."

Doc extended his hand toward Hilliard. Their fingers interlocked. Doc felt the shifting of weight from Hilliard's body. He was trying to pull Doc over into the canyon. Doc let go of his slippery fingers, but the sudden loss of balance sent him tumbling back onto the ground.

Hilliard crawled over the rim of the canyon, struggling to get to his feet. Doc raised the derringer and fired, but he hit only the night air. A silhouette flew down at him from the spectral glow in the sky. Doc rolled left and Hilliard crashed into a mud puddle.

Both men were on their feet, standing toe to toe. Hilliard threw the first punch at Doc, cuffing him on the side of the head. Doc moved with the blow, deflecting the angle, striking back with the ridge of his hand against Hilliard's jaw.

The initial blow incapacitated Hilliard, but Doc did not stop. He pulled out all of his tricks—the Oriental styles, bare knuckles, and the Indian moves that Raider had showed him. He kept Hilliard on his feet with strike after strike, pummeling the fixer of races until he collapsed on the rain-soaked ground.

"Get up, you son of a bitch," Doc cried. "I'll make you pay for what you did to Susanna Bolton."

"Please," Hilliard whimpered. "I didn't do anything to her. Your partner stopped me before I could . . . Please, don't kill me. Don't hit me anymore."

Doc shook his head, trying to clear some of the cobwebs.

He realized that he was holding a large rock in his hands. He had meant it for Dalton Hilliard's head. The rock splashed in a puddle next to Hilliard's face.

Doc rubbed his knuckles. "Can you walk, Hilliard?"

"I don't know, I . . ."

Doc grabbed him under the arms and lifted him to his feet. Hilliard staggered a few feet and fell back into the mud. He raised his arm for Doc to help him up again.

"No you don't, Hilliard. I'm not carrying you back to the train. You can crawl all the way back if you can't walk. So get moving!"

Hilliard was crying like a baby. Doc applied the toe of his shoe to the fallen man's ribs. Hilliard scrambled to his feet in seconds. He started to stumble toward the train, losing his balance, falling, only to have Doc urge him on again.

"You might have to walk all the way back to Carson City," Doc said. "Would you like that, Dalton?"

Hilliard rested on all fours in a pool of standing water. The rain fell in a driving sheet. Doc saw the train ahead of them when the lightning sparked overhead. Hilliard opened his mouth and vomited.

Doc shook his head. "You're the worse type of vermin imaginable, Hilliard. I should have let you fall into the canyon. Get up. Get up before I drag you back there and throw you in myself."

Hilliard managed to right himself. He swayed toward the train, walking in a comic stumble. Doc followed him, thinking that Hilliard wasn't going to cause any more trouble on this godforsaken night.

CHAPTER FOURTEEN

Raider lifted the Colt when Doc opened the compartment door. "You scared the hell out of me, Weatherbee. This storm has got me spooked."

Hilliard's body crumpled in front of Raider, hitting the floor with a wet thud. Raider looked at the man's bleeding wounds as he holstered the Peacemaker. Doc removed his waterlogged jacket, throwing it on top of Hilliard.

Raider frowned a little. "You roughed him up pretty good, Doc."

"I lost my temper."

Raider looked sideways at his partner. "That ain't like you, Doc."

Doc looked down at the girl. "How is she?"

"Runnin' a fever," Raider replied. "I gave her some whiskey and washed her face with cool water."

Doc leaned over Susanna. "You did well, Raider."

The big man scratched his head. "How'd she get sick so fast?"

"Him." Doc pointed at the pitiful figure of Dalton Hilliard. "Get him the hell out of my sight. Put him in the room where he had me."

Raider lifted Hilliard by the armpits. "Come on, boy, we're gonna take you back to Carson City. There's gonna be a lot of people surprised to see you. And I think you're gonna be surprised to—"

"You ain't goin' nowhere but hell, cowboy."

Frank Teal stood in the doorway of the compartment, holding his Winchester. A dried line of blood streaked his face from forehead to jaw. He motioned with the barrel of the rifle.

"Get their guns, Mr. Hilliard."

The frail body stiffened to life. "Frank? Is that really you? I'm not dreaming. Thank God."

Hilliard grabbed Raider's .45 out of his holster. He stepped back and raised the bore at Doc. "The derringer, Weatherbee. Where is it?"

Doc glared at him. "I dropped it in the mud."

Teal leaned forward. "Want me to drop him, boss?"

"Not just yet," Hilliard replied. "I want to make him suffer first. He'll have to pay for this beating he gave me."

"A beating you deserved!" Doc cried.

Hilliard swung the butt of the Colt, hitting Doc in the hard part of the skull. Raider flinched, but the barrel of Teal's Winchester kept him from tearing off Hilliard's head. Hilliard laughed and looked down at Susanna.

"She's a fragile young thing, isn't she, Weatherbee? Too bad she's going to die with you." Hilliard turned toward Teal. "My God, man, where did you come from?"

Teal's dirty face twisted into a jack-o'-lantern grimace. "Big man knocked me off the back of the train. I thought I was done for, but the fall didn't kill me. I got up and walked for a while till this horse come along. A black stallion, brought me up the tracks as fast as the train."

Hilliard looked at Raider. "You were riding Eastern Star, weren't you?"

Raider scowled at the man holding his own gun. "I rode the real Star, fancy man. Not that sham you palmed off on those poor folks in Carson City."

Hilliard smiled weakly. "I have all the money. Do you know Susanna's lying on it? It's under that seat."

Doc held Susanna's head in his hands. "Let her go, Hilliard. Raider and I will be your hostages until you decide to kill us.

But release Susanna at the next station."

"Under no circumstances will any of you go free."

"She's sick, damn it, and you made her that way!"

Hilliard's body trembled. "Then I shall have the pleasure of watching her die. Teal, go forward and tell the engineer and the conductor to get under way at once."

Teal's face turned a dark red. "I can't do that, boss. I killed both of them when I snuck up on the train. Killed all the passengers too, with my knife, so's these Pinkertons wouldn't hear me."

Hilliard glared at his henchmen. "Can't you do anything right, you fool?"

Teal's eyes narrowed. "Don't call me that. Don't call me no fool."

"I can engineer the train," Doc said.

Hilliard and Teal looked at him.

"Why'd you want to help us?" Teal asked.

Doc gestured toward Susanna. "I want to help her, Mr. Teal. If you will let her leave the train at the next stop, I will see to it that you make the Wyoming border by morning."

Raider grabbed Doc's arm. "You can't do this, Doc. These shitbirds ain't gonna let none of us live, no matter what you do."

"What about Susanna, Raider? Do you want her to die?"

Raider looked down at the girl. "Dang it all, why'd you have to get sweet on her, Doc?"

Hilliard laughed. He seemed to be regaining his strength. "So, we have a new engineer for this locomotive. Mr. Weatherbee, shall we go forward?"

"Raider has to come with us," Doc replied. "He can stoke the furnace."

Hilliard nodded. "Very well, but we'll shoot if either one of you makes a tricky move. Lead the way, Pinkerton. We'll see if you're a man of your word."

Eastern Star was tied to the engine, where Teal had left him. Doc and Raider walked through the rain toward the big colt. Some of his black dye had come off in the storm, revealing the chestnut hide underneath. The stallion snorted as Hilliard urged Doc and Raider into the cab of the engine.

Teal gestured toward Raider with the Winchester. "Pick up the shovel, cowboy, and start spoonin' coal into that firebox."

Raider hesitated. "I can't do it, Doc. I can't go along with this. I don't care if they shoot me right here, I ain't helpin' 'em escape."

Doc picked up the shovel himself. "Then I'll do it without you."

Hilliard cocked Raider's Colt, pointing it at Eastern Star. "Help your partner, cowboy, or I'll shoot the horse and then the girl. I'll shoot both of them right in front of you, and you'll have to watch."

Raider pointed his finger at Hilliard. "It takes a sick kinda badger to shoot an innocent animal."

Hilliard laughed. "You mean you've never killed anyone, Raider?"

The big man hung his head. "I've killed my share. But I never liked it. And I only done it in the line of duty."

"I have my duty," Hilliard replied. "Now, do you shovel or do you watch me shoot this fine thoroughbred?"

Raider snatched the coal shovel from Doc. "Don't turn your back on me, Hilliard. I might be ridin' over it if you do."

Doc began to manipulate switches and gadgets in the engineer's cab. "When you killed the engineer, you let the pressure die down in the engine," he said. "It will take about thirty minutes to build up."

Hilliard looked up at the sky. The wind was blowing hard, bringing a lull in the rain. "We can wait, Mr. Weatherbee. We can wait."

Sweat dripped off Raider's forehead as he whispered to his partner, "Why'd you make me do this?"

Doc did not look back from the pressure gauge. "I've got to keep Hilliard from killing us long enough to make a move."

"You two shut up in there."

Teal watched them like a hawk. He was standing next to Eastern Star, drops of water falling off the brim of his hat. The storm had picked up again.

"Hurry up with the engine," Teal cried. "I ain't never seen a rain like this. It keeps startin' and stoppin'."

Raider peered down at him. "Whatta you care, Teal? You

ain't gonna be around much longer. Not if you keep turnin' your back on your boss."

"What do you mean by that, Pinkerton?"

Raider drew his arm over his forehead. "Where's Jimmy Boy, Frank? He ain't here, is he?"

Teal looked sideways at the big man. "He's meetin' us in Kansas City."

Raider laughed sarcastically. "Is that's what you think? Jimmy Boy is sittin' in the Carson City pokey right now. If I was you, I'd be askin' for my cut and clearin' out."

"Shut up, Pinkerton!"

Raider could tell that Teal had started thinking. "How much money has he give you so far, Frank? How much has he promised without deliverin'?"

The rifle lever chortled. "I told you to shut up."

Doc blew the whistle of the train. "I still don't have enough steam pressure to get this thing moving."

Teal turned back toward the private car. "Mr. Hilliard, he said he can't go for a while."

Teal's boss, clad in a fresh white suit, sauntered out of the private car sporting a fancy umbrella to ward off the large drops of rain. He picked a careful path around the mud puddles and came up next to the cab.

"Mr. Weatherbee," Hilliard said, "you haven't been able to get us moving, and it's been well over thirty minutes. Perhaps you were lying to me when you said you could run this train."

Doc leaned over the pressure gauge. "I'm sorry, but your man was responsible for letting the engine cool off."

Hilliard turned toward Teal. "You clumsy saddle tramp! Don't you ever tire of being such a fool?"

Teal turned the Winchester on his employer. "I told you never to call me that. I'm your partner."

Hilliard's eyes were wide open. "Yes, of course . . . partner. Yes, I didn't mean to call you—"

"And you're gonna give me my money, ain't you?" Teal continued.

"Certainly," Hilliard replied. "But I thought we'd wait until we're in Kansas City so Jimmy Boy can—"

Teal stuck the rifle barrel in Hilliard's chest. "I want my money now. My whole cut. And then I'm ridin' out."

"Assuredly, Frank. Assuredly."

Teal turned in a half circle, keeping Hilliard in front of him. Eastern Star whinnied as the white-suited man backed into him. Hilliard felt the thoroughbred against his body.

"You stay right here," Teal said. "When I get my money, you can handle both of these Pinkertons yourself."

"Don't worry, Frank," Hilliard replied with a smile. "You know where the money is. Take all you want. Just leave me some to get by on."

Teal leered at his former boss. "Now you're thinkin' straight."

Teal started for the private car, leaving his back uncovered. Hilliard raised the Colt .45 from under his coat. The Peacemaker barked twice, sending both slugs into Teal's back.

At the sound of the gunshots, Eastern Star spooked, lifting his front legs off the ground. When his hooves fell back to earth, they caught Dalton Hilliard squarely on the head. As he fell, Star continued to stomp him, driving iron shoes into his face and neck.

Raider grabbed Star's reins, pulling him away from Hilliard's twitching corpse. Doc leaned over to examine the crushed gray pulp that had been Hilliard's skull. He had to look away from the bloody mess.

"Star took his head off."

Raider patted the horse's neck. "Saved us a lot of trouble, boy."

Doc stood up and gazed toward the rear of the train. Thunder rolled over the plain as the worst part of the storm came on them. There was no sense going on, not without a crew and passengers.

"Let's try to back her into Hope Junction," Doc said. "Keep stoking the fire. I'll check on Susanna before I try to sort out this mess."

"You do that, Doc."

The man from Boston was sore and soggy as he strode toward the last car on the train. Raider jumped back into the cab, throwing open the door to the firebox. He didn't even look at the bodies on the wet ground. He had seen plenty of dead men in his time, men who had died by his own hand.

He picked up the coal shovel and fed fuel to the raging flames of the orange fire.

CHAPTER FIFTEEN

Judge Brady Farnsworth, First Circuit and District Court, State of Nevada, sat in his ceremonious black robes, glaring suspiciously at Doc Weatherbee. It was a hot day in Carson City, especially with a full courtroom of spectators, mostly bettors who were waiting to see if they would get paid on their bets from the Comstock Stakes. Farnsworth had been listening patiently, sweating out the story for nearly a half hour. Now his gray eyebrows were pointed in and he had a skeptical gleam in his eyes.

"Mr. Weatherbee, let me see if I can get this straight. You're tellin' me that a man named Hilliard sponsored this race with a man named Bolton, so he could cheat everyone by switchin' horses?"

"Correct. He palmed off a fake horse as the favorite, disguising the real Eastern Star as a long shot. When the long-odds horse won, Hilliard was able to abscond with the large betting pool on the favorite. He was even able to leave enough money to pay most of the bets on the long shot, Ebony Cat."

The judge nodded. "Ebony Cat, which was the real Eastern Star."

"I believe you have it straight, sir."

Farnsworth's eyes fell on Raider. "Ain't heard much from you, boy."

"It's just like Doc said it," Raider replied.

Farnsworth threw up his hands. "Where's this Bolton now, Weatherbee?"

"Dead."

"And Hilliard?" the judge said to Raider.

Raider's face turned bright red. "I guess he's dead too, Judge Farnsworth. But we didn't kill him. The horse did it. See, he kidnapped this girl and . . ."

The judge shook his head. "There's a girl in this. I mighta knowed."

"Yes," Doc replied, "Susanna Bolton, Jacob Bolton's daughter."

The judge gestured toward the courtroom. "Is she here?"

"No," Doc replied. "She's not feeling well right now. But she can appear before you when she's better."

Farnsworth gave it consideration. "Well, let's go on without her for now. Who's that man smokin' a pipe in this courtroom?"

Somebody in the gallery yelled out, "He's the jockey that threw the race. String him up."

Everyone howled with laughter. The judge brought down his gavel, restoring order with a warning of eviction for any further outbursts. Then he peered down at Zebulon Freeman.

"Is it true that you cheated in this race?" the judge asked.

"No, sir, I rode Eastern Star, the fake one that is, at the request of Mr. Weatherbee." Freeman looked back at Doc.

The man from Boston picked up his cue. "Yes, sir, as part of the investigation, I had to determine if the horses had indeed been switched. Mr. Freeman was able to confirm that suspicion for me. He cooperated with us completely. I can vouch for his character."

The judge softened a little. "All right, that's enough from you for now, Freeman. Weatherbee, you say this man Hilliard ran off with a pile of money. You know where that money is?"

Doc lifted a carpet suitcase onto the judge's bench. "Right here, Your Honor."

A cheer went up through the crowd. Farnsworth was forced to use his gavel again. When things were hushed, he leaned over toward Doc.

"What do you want me to do here, Weatherbee?"

"The money for winning bets on Eastern Star must be distributed."

Farnsworth shrugged. "I ain't no race steward. Don't you have a judge for this thing?"

"Er, yes," Doc replied.

Farnsworth gazed into the crowd. "Is the judge here?"

After a moment, the old man stepped forward. Farnsworth seemed to recognize him. "Why, hello, Judge Benbow. Don't tell me you're mixed up in this thing!"

Benbow hung his head a little. "Reckon I am, Brady. They offered me fifty dollars if I'd do it."

Farnsworth smiled and nodded. "Well, you ain't a judge no more, so I can't hold it against you."

"Thank you, Brady."

Farnsworth locked his hands together. "Judge Benbow, you was the steward on this race. Did you hand down a ruling?"

Benbow held up his hand. "I did. Them that bet on Eastern Star will get paid their winnin's, since these Pinkertons proved that the real Eastern Star won by bein' disguised."

Farnsworth banged his gavel. "Then let it be done. Bailiff, take this money and pay every marker bet on Eastern Star."

The crowd started to cheer.

"Outside!" Farnsworth cried. "Take the money outside."

There was a rush onto the street. Farnsworth waited for the courtroom to clear before he called Doc and Raider up to his bench. The judge seemed a little tentative.

"Gentlemen, you come in here tellin' me about bettin' and dead men and horses bein' painted. Somethin' makes me think that you might be back here to see me before this whole thing is over."

Doc smiled reassuringly. "I'll file a report of the case with you, Judge Farnsworth. Believe it or not, my partner and I didn't kill anyone in this case—which is quite unusual, especially for my partner."

The judge glared at the big man. "You know anything about them dead Indians that was brung in last week?"

"Well, sir," Raider started, "as a matter of fact—"

Farnsworth held up his palms. "Stop right there. Don't tell me no more about it. Just clear on out of here."

Doc took an envelope out of his pocket. "Judge, before we

go, I wanted to give you this. Inside you'll find the document that chartered the horse race. It's quite illegal. The sponsor of the document is a senator in the state legislature. If you are an honest man, you'll know what to do with this information."

The judge took the envelope from Doc's hand. "Well now, that is an interestin' piece of news. I reckon you Pinkertons are as good as they say you are."

"Of course," Doc said, "if you say that I gave you the document, I will have to deny it. Our agency is never inclined to become mixed up in government affairs, state or otherwise."

Raider grabbed Doc's shoulder and spun him around quickly. "Judge, I'm gonna get him out of here before he talks us into some more trouble. Thank you for bein' so fair."

"Out!" Farnsworth cried. "And stay away from Carson City as long as you can!"

He didn't have to tell them twice.

Doc stood at the edge of the corral, watching Susanna Bolton as she groomed Eastern Star. She had recovered from her fever and was looking quite beautiful, Doc thought, even though she was wearing her man-tailored suit to hide the curves of her body. The lady was holding up well in spite of everything. Doc wished he could spend some more time with her.

"Hello, Susanna."

She turned around quickly to face him. Her face slacked into a frown. She spun back and ran the comb over Star's flank.

"You'll get your fee, Mr. Weatherbee. As soon as I have a penny to my name. I'm taking Star back east to race. Freeman thinks we can win a lot of money."

Doc held his derby in his hands, trying to be easy on her. "Susanna, I haven't come about our fee. In fact, I have some rather extraordinary news for you."

She peered tentatively over her shoulder. "Good news? For me? I've had so little of that these days."

Doc lifted a small book out of his pocket. "This is a savings account in your name at a bank in Carson City. Seven thousand dollars."

Susanna's green eyes were wide with disbelief. "Are you telling me the truth, Doc? Don't toy with me about something like this."

Doc threw the bankbook to her. "I did some checking while you were recovering. Hilliard was a good manager, it seems. The Comstock Stakes showed a profit of nearly twenty thousand. I entrusted the bank with the earnings, and they proceeded to clear up all of your father's debts, including the fee to our agency."

She started to cry. "Oh, Doc, I'm sorry I snapped at you."

He hugged her close to him. "I also spoke with the surveyor at Western Dominion Mining, the man who used to work for your father. He said that two of the dry gold mines show rich deposits of lead and mercury. Not as profitable as gold, but Western Dominion may offer to buy the two mines from you at a substantial rate."

She gazed up into his eyes. "Doc, I have an idea. Why don't you come with me? I'll hire you to take Star back east."

"I'm sorry, Susanna. Raider and I have already been assigned to another case. We'll be leaving in the morning."

She sighed. "I think a great deal of you, Doc."

He took her hands. "Susanna, you have my full respect. I hope you know that. If I were another kind of man, I might ask you to . . . that is, things might be different."

"But you're not another kind of man, Doc. You're a great deal more."

He kissed her softly on the lips. Star snorted behind them.

Susanna laughed for the first time. "I think Star's jealous of you, Doc."

He touched her face. "If you're agreeable, Susanna, I'd like to have dinner with you at the hotel tonight."

"Of course," she replied. "But I've got to groom Star first. Would you like to help?"

Doc picked up the comb. "Yes, I wanted to show you the correct way to do it. You see, you bring the brush down this way . . ."

"Doc . . . I'll never forget you."

He hesitated for a moment, smiling at her. Then he started to drag the comb over the flank of Eastern Star, taking it slowly so he could give Susanna Bolton her lesson.

Raider sat on the corral next to Zeb Freeman, watching Doc and the girl as they fussed over the horse.

Raider shook his head. "I guess that ole boy is worth all the pamperin'. I never rode one finer or faster. He ran for me when I needed him."

Freeman lowered a match to the bowl of his pipe. "I hear Jimmy Boy Johnson got three months on a work gang."

"Territorial prison might kill him," Raider replied.

Freeman looked sideways at the big man. "Hear you wagered on Ebony Cat."

Raider laughed. "Only after Doc showed me the truth. I knew I was wagerin' on Star. Hell, after that old judge ruled, I was shit out of luck."

They were quiet for a minute, trying not to notice that Doc was kissing Susanna.

"Guess I ain't gonna bet too much on racin' anymore," Raider said. "Unless you're ridin' and Star's runnin'."

Freeman nodded. "Gonna be a lot of that back east. I'm gonna do Miss Susanna proud. We're gonna win a few purses."

"I'm gonna stick to blackjack," Raider said. "Horses and me don't get along too good."

Freeman stared down the railing of the corral. "Looks like you got one friend, Raider."

Star's companion, the black cat, sauntered slowly toward them along the rail.

"Where'd that thing come from?" Raider scowled.

Freeman smiled. "He just wants to be your amigo."

"Wants to bring me bad luck."

"Don't be so superstitious," Freeman said. "He just wants you to pet him. Go on."

Raider stretched out his hand to rub the black cat on top of the head. The feline arched a furry back and hissed at Raider, ripping a sharp set of claws across his arm. Raider lost his balance and tumbled off the railing into a horse trough. The big man just sat there, disgusted with himself.

Freeman laughed so hard he almost fell off the fence. "Dang me, Raider, if you don't have the worse luck of any man I ever seen."

"It's gonna change. And soon, I hope."

"How do you know that?"

Raider splashed water in his face. "It's got to change, Freeman. It's just got to."

EPILOGUE

Raider pulled the slender blond woman closer to him, lifting the whiskey bottle to his lips. He drank a healthy swallow and wiped his mouth with the back of his hand. The woman, Sally Jane, saw the scar on his hand. She ran her fingertips across the hardened tissue.

"I didn't see this in bed, Raider. When did you hurt yourself?"

The tall man shrugged. "About five months ago, in Nevada."

Sally Jane gazed out at the parade of horses that walked by them. "How long you been in Waco, honey?"

"I been waitin' for my partner for three days. He's comin' up from Brownsville. He should be here by tomorrow afternoon at the latest."

Sally Jane reached for the bottle herself. "What work do you do, cowboy?"

Raider laughed and tipped back his Stetson. "I poke around in other people's business. Just like a old washerwoman. Hey, don't drink all of that. Leave a little for me."

She wiped her face on his shirt. "Well, I sure don't know

what you're doin' here in Waco."

Raider glanced up over the reviewing stand, keeping an eye on the big clock. He had arrived just in time for the quarter-horse races. They were smaller than Eastern Star, and built for running a quarter mile as fast as any animal on the continent.

"Why the hell did you bring me out here, anyway?" said Sally Jane.

"Aw, quit yer bitchin'. Ain't nobody in town to need your services. You wouldn't whore-up any money this afternoon. Besides, if you get the right bet down . . . look at that!"

Prancing toward them was a bone-white stallion with Jimmy Boy Johnson in the saddle. Johnson had survived the prison work gang. He had somehow got out and found the Indian pony. Now he was about to run against some of Texas's finest steeds. And he had a good chance of winning.

Johnson looked frightened when he saw Raider. A wink from the big man's black eye put him at ease. Raider wasn't going to turn him in. He was going to wager on him.

"Where's the bet-taker, Sally?"

Her lower lip was a coral pout. "I ain't seen it. Raider, take me back to town, I ain't a bit interested in—"

He put his hand on her shoulder. "If you don't hush up, I'm gonna run your ass all the way back to town. Now I'm goin' to put down a bet. If you want to come on, I got a sure thing."

She folded her arms for a long sulking. "I ain't gonna waste any of my money."

Raider leaned down and kissed her ear. "You're gonna get all of my winnin's anyway. You'll take 'em from me in bed."

A portly man in a cheap derby took Raider's bet on "Western Star," giving him ten-to-one odds. His eyes bulged when Raider took out five double eagles and creased them in his hand.

The portly man sneezed nervously. "A hundred dollars. I would have to pay you a thousand."

Raider patted the bookmaker's coat pocket. "Looks like you had a good day. If you don't want to take my bet, I'll find somebody else . . ."

"I never refuse a bet, sir. It's done."

He gave Raider a marker with his personal seal on it. Raider strode back toward the finish line, passing the sign that read,

"No Gambling." Well, he thought, they did things a little different in Texas.

Sally Jane was still pouting when he got back. If she didn't give it up, he was going to switch to the fat girl down the hall. She had a bigger chest anyway. Sally Jane perked up a little when she heard the trumpet calling the horses to the starting line.

"Is it going to be over?" she asked.

"In a minute or so," Raider replied.

The starter fired a small-caliber pistol to begin the race. Raider watched the flash of white as Western Star eased into second place. Johnson wasn't taking any chances with his ringer. He stayed close to the pack all the way to the top of the stretch. Then he gave the Indian pony his head, and he drove home to win the quarter-mile race by fifty feet.

"Did you win?" Sally Jane cried.

Raider saw the cheap derby bobbing through the crowd. He managed to intercept the bookie before he got away. The fat man dangled from Raider's hand, shuddering in his shoes.

Raider smiled like a good ole boy. "You wasn't plannin' to weasel out on me without payin', were you?"

"Oh no," the fat man replied, reaching into his coat pocket. "Here you go, one thousand. I counted it out."

Raider took the roll of script from his chubby fingers. "Much obliged, sir. Much obliged."

Sally Jane came up behind him, grumbling until she saw the wad of bills.

"You did *win!*"

Raider slid his hand over her tight bottom. "You want some of this, Sally?"

She pressed her body into his. "You know I do."

Raider grinned. "Then let's go back into town and see how much of it you can earn."

They climbed into the seat of Sally Jane's buggy. As they rolled toward the dirt road leading back to town, Raider saw Jimmy Boy Johnson pulling the Indian pony on a short tether. Johnson looked pretty good for a man who had spent time in a territorial prison. Raider waved him the high sign and kept on going toward Waco. Johnson wasn't doing anything illegal—not so's you'd notice, anyway. And didn't a fellow have a right to make himself a living?

"Whoo wee," said Sally Jane, "I don't like the races, but I sure like winning."

"You ain't the only one."

"Umm, Raider..."

She ran her hands over his crotch. Raider felt the stiffening in his denim pants. Sally Jane put her tongue in his ear.

"You better stop that, lady, or I'm liable to pull over and top you right here on this road."

Sally Jane bit his earlobe. "It'll cost you twenty-five dollars if you want it in the buggy."

Raider pulled back the reins, stopping the vehicle. His hands went for the buttons of his fly. Sally Jane hiked up her dress, spreading her long legs. She reached up to stroke the bare length of Raider's manhood.

Sally Jane smiled. "I know why you do so good with horses."

"Why's that?"

"Because you're hung like one."

Raider fell between her legs, impaling her with his shaft. Sally Jane cried out with each thrust. The springs of the buggy continued squeaking well into the coolness of late afternoon.